Mr Tolly of Greenwi(

By Colin Walpole

By the Same Author

A World without Money or Politicians

The Lives and Deaths of Terry Toft

Experimenting with Short Stories

Contents

Introduction

One never knows quite what to expect when visiting my brother Ron. Despite being challenged physically and having a pre-war birth certificate he has a youthful disposition and a keen sense of irony.
I popped in to see him one day and he recalled an incident in the garden which triggered a whole new adventure. This is it.

Trapped

Pidgin English

Ron was dozing in his wheelchair in the garden when he became acutely aware of the presence of another being. He was neither asleep nor awake but temporarily suspended at that special place where mind games tease and fantasy rules. Even for a confused moment, unsure whether he had been falling asleep or waking up.

'What's that kerfuffle?' He grunted. Other *beings* – human or otherwise – were mostly a nuisance and to be avoided.

Ron's activities included reading and doing the crossword in the newspaper but his main pastime was observing the many birds that visited his garden to feed.

'There's something behind that pot.' He watched and waited, expecting a squirrel, a hedgehog or perhaps a bird to emerge. Bird feeders hung from the trees and bushes, they were full of seeds and nuts and fat-balls dangled alongside. Sparrows came to feed, blue tits, starlings all types of birds. But not only birds, squirrels and even tiny field mice enjoyed Ron's hospitality from time to time.

'It might be a mouse or a *rat*, blast, it sounds big enough to be a rat,' he lowered his voice.

'I had better take a closer look.' He released the brakes on the wheelchair and inched towards the pot, in which a young bay tree grew. The newspaper on his lap with the half-finished crossword slid to the ground obscuring the area which he had hoped to view.

He pulled it aside and came face to face with his uninvited guest.

'A pigeon! You poor little chap, don't worry I'll soon have you out of there.' This was no ordinary pigeon – this was Mr Tolly.

Ron heaved himself up and grabbed his walking frame. He wanted to see how the pigeon was trapped and pulled the bay tree gently to one side and peered down.

'Aha, you're tangled in those twigs, I'll have to shift the pot and that won't be easy.' He manoeuvred into a stronger position mumbling, 'if it's not one thing it's another, lunch time soon and I'm hungry.'

Ron tugged at the earthenware pot.

'Oh, you silly fat pigeon, take a step back and you'll be free from that twig around your neck.' He watched and waited to see if the bird could wriggle free.

'No – backwards, stop pushing forward, you're making it worse. I had better fetch the secateurs from the shed.'

He set off at a pace for the shed, paused, turned around and, on passing the pot, explained that he had forgotten the key.

The little bird heard from the kitchen, 'now where's that key? Ah yes, the bureau, top drawer.'

He whizzed by the pot again. The aluminium walking frame rattled its loose bolt and showed signs of overheating.

'Shan't be long now – *she'll be comin' round the mountain when she comes tra la la.'*

Mr Tolly heard hand tools falling from the shelf and the lawnmower's wheels scraping on the floor as Ron searched for the secateurs.

'Oh blast they're no good.'

On his way back to the kitchen, he shouted, 'the secateurs were all rusted up. No good. I'll fetch a knife from the kitchen. Not long now. Don't go away.'

He eventually approached the pot breathless, muttering something about pigeons not being able to walk backwards and that he had never seen one walking backwards, or flying in reverse for that matter.

'I'm walking backwards to Christmas, across the Irish sea ...'

He reached carefully towards the 'V'-shaped twig that had trapped the little bird.

'Now keep still, don't fidget like that, this knife is extremely sharp, one false move and I'll have your head off. That's better, this won't hurt, you won't feel a thing, it'll all be over soon and then I can have my lunch.' Luckily, Mr Tolly did not understand these words. Had he, he would have taken sparse comfort from them.

The knife was but a gnat's whisker from Mr Tolly's neck and the offending twig.

'Stop all that flapping, you're sending feathers and dust everywhere. What if I should sneeze?'

Ron sneezed. The knife sliced through the twig and Mr Tolly flew to freedom.

He watched the bird fly along the garden and over the fence towards the allotments.

'Stupid bird, all that flapping, I could have had his head off.' He had his lunch (not pigeon pie) then settled in his wheelchair to finish the crossword and enjoy the afternoon sun.

'Now let me see – *9 down: abridged language 6 and 7*.'

He fought the lunch-induced drowsiness and began to relive the rescue.

'How grateful that little fat pigeon must be. Had I not been in the garden, a rat might have eaten him – a cat might have eaten the rat – a fox might have eaten the cat.' He was at that special place again. 'A tiger might have eaten the fox – an elephant might have eaten the mouse – the mouse might have eaten the house – the house might have eaten – zzz,' his head lolled forward onto his chest.

*

Now, Mr Tolly was a resilient fellow and, although frightened during his captivity, he took comfort from the fact that he had outwitted his captor. A less resourceful bird may have conceded defeat and ended up in a pie. His daring escape would provide the plot for a bedtime story for his two young chicks Alf and Crispin.

Mr Tolly's bedtime stories were epic. Neighbouring pigeons often gathered to enjoy them, too. The wide beam under the railway bridge by Greenwich Railway Station was quite a little *pigeon theatre* at bedtime.

*

'I have special story for you tonight because it's based on a true event.'

The 20.05 to Charing Cross rumbled on into London. Alf and Crispin huddled together in the nest, Mrs Tolly and several neighbours settled down to listen.

'Whilst foraging for food in a garden today, I was lured into a trap.'

'Coo.'

'Don't you overexcite the chicks, Mr Tolly, it's bedtime.'

'A cunning trap in a garden not far from here. A lesser pigeon would have succumbed and become pie meat.'

'Cooo.'

'That was the plan, I'm sure. The trap lay between a low retaining wall and an earthenware pot disguised, as a ... as an earthenware pot. The space between narrowed and narrowed until I could progress no more, I had eaten my way into the trap and found myself shackled by the neck. Further movement was impossible. The gap was too small.'

'Or you were too wide,' said Mrs Tolly.

'On noticing that the trap had been triggered, the man stirred from his chariot, snorting and uttering hungry sounds. His first attempt at securing me with a paper net failed, sending him into a rage. He dashed, first this way – for tools of execution – then that way to the kitchen for his spear. He chanted curses in that melodic way humans sometime do and talked of his hunger and meal time. My chances of survival were nil. I waited patiently for death. '

'Coooo.'

'It was clear, he was intent on making a pie – with me as the key ingredient.'

'Not worried about his cholesterol levels then?' chuckled Mrs Tolly.

Four large round chick eyes went from their father to their mother and back again. The 20.15 carried workers homeward.

'All of a sudden, and under the pressure of my forward motion, I sensed the pot moving. With one tremendous heave from my mighty wing, I pushed the pot aside – released some downy feathers – flapped my wings, which sent dust and feathers into the air and up his nose, inducing a fit of sneezing. I sidestepped the blade which sliced through the manacles, enabling my escape. Pigeon outwits man. And I'm alive and well to prove that the story is true.'

Mr Tolly extended his body to take a deep bow and Mrs Tolly saw the missing feathers from around his neck. She took off and joined him at his side. The audience clapped their wings and took off in a pandemonium of excitement while a London-bound train clattered above.

Alf and Crispin slept. Mr and Mrs Tolly gazed upon them and drank in their beauty, the bulging eyes, the grey wrinkly skin hairy and half feathered. Mrs Tolly puffed herself up and wriggled between them spreading her wings protectively to warm them. She glanced at the hero of the moment.

'You need to lose weight, getting stuck like that.'

'It was a trap.' He shook his head. 'Tut tut … I can never win. I might as well make myself comfortable.' So he tucked his head under his wing, stood on one leg and with a sigh said.

'Good night.'

Darkness took hold and the 20.45 went to another place.

Elvis Whites

Elvis was away the night that Mr Tolly told the story of his capture and escape. He was curious to hear the whole episode from Mr Tolly himself.

'Tell me about it on the way to the park,' he said.

Mr Tolly was attending to his chicks.

'I'll tell you when we get to the park, I can't fly and talk. I'm not as fit as I used to be.'

'Mrs Tolly returned and landed delicately by the nest. Mr Tolly moved to let her feed the chicks. She looked suspiciously at Elvis, then at her husband.

'What are you up to, Elvis?' She asked accusingly.

'Good morning Mrs Tolly. Nothing, just planning a trip to the park with Mr Tolly. I'll wait up top.' He launched from the beam, looped upwards and landed on the ticket office roof.

He watched the 7.31 to London Bridge as it moved slowly out of the station, jam-packed with humans.

'Poor things,' Elvis thought. 'I wonder what they've done. They must have been very naughty.'

'He's a ne'er-do-well,' ranted Mrs Tolly, 'I knew he'd be around.'

'He means no harm, he's a good pigeon at heart,' said Mr Tolly.

'You be careful.'

Mr Tolly and Elvis flew to Greenwich Park and landed in the flower gardens. They walked towards the duck pond and began feeding on bread crumbs.

Mr Tolly retold his account of the events in the garden, he enjoyed telling the story of his capture and courageous escape, *'the big white net ... the pigeon pie ... the enormous knife,'* embellishing here, and exaggerating a little there ... *'one tremendous push from my mighty wing'.*

Mr Tolly had finished his story with a flourish and now waited for Elvis's reaction. Elvis did not speak, without a word or a coo, he flew to the upper branches of a tall conker tree. Mr Tolly followed and landed next to him.

'I'm gonna *white* him!' Said Elvis.

Now it was Mr Tolly's turn to be silent but it wasn't by choice. Mr Tolly was so shocked at the idea of *whiting* the old man that, for a moment, he could not speak at all.

'No no, not that, *whiting* is forbidden, *whiting* is not allowed. It's strictly against bird protocol, don't even consider it.'

Elvis was not listening and his eyes narrowed as he focused on a distant memory that caused him pain.

'He deserves it, you might have ended up in a pie and you have a family to care for. Just show me the garden and the target, you need no further involvement.

Now Mr Tolly was not listening. They were not listening to each other.

Mr Tolly was shaking and rambling on about it being illegal and about him being a highly respectable member of society and what if Mrs Tolly found out?

He flew off.

Elvis pulled alongside. 'Lead me to the garden, show me the old man.'

'No, no.'

'Or Mrs Tolly might hear about Dora,' Elvis whispered. 'Meet me in the park, same time tomorrow.'

Elvis landed gently on the 8.45 to London Bridge. 'That pigeon is chicken,' he said to himself. He, on the other hand was not, he was off to meet his friend, the sparrow hawk, Mercedes.

Mr Tolly landed clumsily on the beam next to the nest.

'I don't feel well. I think I ate too much bread' he said. But Mrs Tolly sensed his agitation, she also knew any cross-examination would shed no light and so she left Mr Tolly to look after Alf and Crispin.

He fed them absent-mindedly and rather than carefully transferring the milky substance gently into their open beaks, he vomited everywhere missing the target.

He manoeuvred on to the nest to keep the chicks warm.

'Oops, sorry,' he trod on Alf's head then nearly pushed Crispin out of the nest.

'*Whiting*? Dora? How did he know about Dora, nobody knew about Dora? I did not even know her name until Elvis said it.' Dora was a ring dove whom he admired from afar. He had never even spoken to her.

'He must have seen me looking at her. Dora,' he mused, 'yes she looks like a Dora.'

Mr Tolly knew his dear wife would believe Elvis if he told her about Dora. His heart sunk, he was in trouble. He recalled her words from earlier in the day *'you be careful',* 'well, I was careful. I was boastful when telling Elvis my story, but this was *Elvis* and he was hanging on my every word.'

***

The mystic art of whiting, in addition to being outlawed, was quite difficult. Speed, stomach pressure, prevailing weather conditions, thermals and diet all had an impact on accuracy.

In Greenwich Park, Elvis was practicing. His initial target was the statue of James Wolfe, then progressing to waste bins, which were smaller and more challenging.

To keep other birds at bay, he had Mercedes in attendance. To be seen practicing whiting might link him to the crime he was planning. A sparrow hawk would keep most birds at bay.

She perched high in a tree, watching his every move. She thought him handsome, how athletic and distinctive he looked with his white and grey markings, a show-off certainly. He enjoyed the speed of the swoop, the sound of his wing feathers squeaking as he flexed them against the wind.

Mercedes launched and followed him into a dive; in contrast her wings beat with a deathly silence, he was unaware of her, her softly feathered legs came forward, talons spread like grabbing hands, the distance between them narrowed, Elvis neared the target and fired. Bull's eye, he turned and saw her face, a strangely intense face that he hardly recognised.

Alarmed by her powerful instinct, she pulled out of her deadly trajectory and headed for the trees.

'That was close.'

'Close? It was dead centre.'

'Let's catch a train back to my place,' suggested Mercedes.

'Not yet' said Elvis with a glint in his eye. 'I want a shot at a moving target.'

'A deer?'

'No.'

'A car?'

'No. Come on. Follow me.'

They made their way across the park to the cricket pitch where a game was in progress. The unlikely pair watched for a while from a low mulberry tree at the edge of the boundary.

'I thought you said a *moving* target' said Mercedes.

'Human behaviour is very interesting', said Elvis 'they're punished by being packed into trains and moved slowly about on shiny rails ... these must be the more serious offenders.'

They watched more of the cricket match, 'but look, they *do* move. They chase that ball and throw it around in a random fashion.'

'How strange.'

'OK, I think I have it,' Elvis was planning an attack. 'Do you see that white line encircling the punishment area?'

'Yes, I do see it, I'm a hawk.'

'Of course, well, there are no birds inside that circle. If you race around the outside and create a diversion, I'll try to white one of the men as they chase the ball.'

'Clockwise or anticlockwise.'

'Just do it ... twice to be certain.'

His eyes followed her flight, the long tail and short rounded wings, her twisting turning movements, dipping low before rising over the bushes and trees. It was working, blackbirds were dashing for cover and spreading their warning.

As Mercedes passed overhead for her second lap, he launched from the cover of the mulberry tree and positioned himself over the cricket pitch. He focused on the miscreants below.

The batsman parried a spinning ball harmlessly into the ground. Elvis watched from above. The ball made its way back to the bowling end. The bowler started his short run. This time, the batsman had his measure; he stepped forward and took it on the full, middle of the bat, along the ground towards the boundary. Square leg gave chase and so did Elvis, at full speed. The fielder was about ten yards from the ball, which was moving at a pace towards the boundary. Elvis followed the same line, then slowed and rotated his wings to break his speed, simultaneously bringing his undercarriage forward, he fired, *squidge – splat.* A direct hit, ear, shoulder and back, white on white.

'Not bad,' he looked up and saw Mercedes above him, hovering, as if clapping.

'Let's go,' he called. 'Race you to the rail track.'

The ball trickled over the boundary, the batsmen returned to their creases. Whilst the fielding side fell about laughing, the victim wiped his ear and twisted his head to inspect the damage.

One umpire said to the other 'I know it sounds daft, but I'm sure that pigeon did that with wilful intent.'

'I agree' said the other, signalling a four, 'it does sound daft.'

*

At Greenwich Park next day Mr Tolly agreed to show Elvis the garden. He had little choice.

'OK, OK, I'll take you to the garden, just promise to keep quiet about Dora.'

They flew over the park wall and made their way to the allotments at the rear of Ron's garden. They landed together on the back fence.

'This is it. There are the seed containers and you can see the fat-balls designed to lure innocent birds to their death. I bet he lives on pigeon pie, him in there, in that house, him, that man, that ... Elvis, this is no laughing matter. Why are you laughing?'

'You don't fly in this area very much, do you?'

'Well not since – not much before that either, in fact, only the once.'

'All that practice for nothing,' said Elvis. 'This is Ron's garden. He's famous around here for feeding us birds.'

Mr Tolly Sings

'You became trapped whilst foraging for food. Correct?' Said Elvis.

'Might've done.'

'And Ron rescued you. Correct?'

'Perhaps.'

'So, instead of being a monster, he's a kind, considerate hero. Correct?'

'Maybe.'

'And you know the reward for humans who are especially kind to birds?'

'Yes I do Elvis. Birdsong. But I'm a pigeon and pigeons can't sing. You must agree with me on that point. A singing pigeon would hardly be reward enough for a fellow like Ron. More of a punishment, have you ever heard me sing?'

'We have to find a way.'

'What do you suggest? Singing lessons?'

'Mr Tolly, return to your chicks, there's someone I know who might be able to help. Let's meet again tomorrow in the park by the cricket pitch. And for the time being we'll keep this between the two of us.'

*

Mr Tolly was right, of course, pigeons are not famous for their singing. But for the sake of good form, Ron had to be rewarded for his gallant act. Elvis searched the ancient Oxleas Woods at the top of Shooters Hill.

He found Justin talking to a robin in a holly bush. They flew to a high branch of an ash tree and Elvis briefed Justin – a blackbird famed for his extraordinary singing voice.

'We'll need to rehearse' said Justin. 'I know a beautiful spring love song, and if this Mr Tolly isn't completely tone deaf, he should be able to mime along.'

'Mm, a love song – look Justin this won't get Mr Tolly into deeper trouble, will it? I visualise pigeon hens throwing themselves at his feet.'

'You know nothing of the birds and the bees, Elvis. Don't worry, just leave it to me.'

Rehearsals were arranged for the next day in Greenwich Park at the cricket pitch.

'Mercedes will take care of security.' Explained Elvis.

'Well, make sure she has eaten.' Said Justin.

The next day the three birds met at the centre of the cricket ground.

'No punishment regime today, I see.' Said Elvis. Mr Tolly absentmindedly ate some grass while Justin warmed up his vocal cords.

'Are we ready for the rehearsal then?'

'Where is your sparrow hawk friend?' Asked Justin.

'I'm not exactly sure but there are no other birds in sight, so she's doing her job. Shall we begin? Maestro, sing!'

Mr Tolly began cooing loudly.

'No, no, no! Not you, Mr Tolly – Justin.'

Justin, who had inhaled a lungful of air deflated like a balloon at the sound of the discordant cooing.

'Let's start again,' said Elvis, 'blackbird sing – pigeon listen.'

Justin gathered himself once more, left wing on stomach, right wing outstretched. His love song rang through the park – Mercedes perched in the mulberry tree spellbound – humans stood – dogs sat and the squirrels suspended their fidgeting for the duration.

'Perfect', said Elvis, 'now it's your turn Mr Tolly.'

He cooed. And, to give him credit he cooed a little more passionately than before. Elvis and Justin looked at each other.

'This isn't going to be easy', breathed Elvis. He explained slowly and clearly to Mr Tolly that this was not a duet and that his role was to stand on the fence and mime – 'you open and close your beak silently in time with the song and make similar movements to

Justin's – Justin stands behind the fence, out of sight, and sings. Ron looks up to see where the music is coming from and sees you singing.'

'But I can't sing.'

'Precisely! That's why we have Justin behind the fence singing. Ron sees you and hears Justin.'

Mr Tolly's eyes widened and he proclaimed thoughtfully.

'You know? That's very clever.' Once he got the hang of it, Mr Tolly was quite good at mimicking the wing movements and opening and closing his beak in time with Justin.

Towards the end of the fourth rendition, Mercedes swooped down and landed amongst them. The three birds scattered instinctively but landed immediately on realising that it was Mercedes. Mr Tolly and Justin took cover behind Elvis – just in case.

'Are you soon finished? I can't control all those hen blackbirds.' She turned to Justin. 'It doesn't do much for me, but those chicks are going wild.'

'Let's check out Ron's garden, the weather's ideal. Mercedes you follow at a safe distance. Let's go.'

*

The three alighted on the fence. Ron was in the garden filling the seed containers.

'Are you ready?' Asked Elvis. They nodded.

'Good, let's do this. I'll get Mercedes to clear the allotment area and I'll watch out for cats.'

The conditions were perfect, quiet, no lawn mowers, a few gardeners at the far side of the allotments. The only disturbance was the scattering birds as Mercedes swept through. Justin was perched behind the fence out of view. Mr Tolly was in position looking out towards the allotments and checking the final details with Justin.

Everyone was ready. Elvis swooped down and landed on the garden shed so that he could see them both yet remain unseen to Ron. He was to conduct.

'Ready?'
'Ready.'
'Turn around and face Ron.'
'Right ... OK ... of course.'

Ron was busily hanging fresh fat-balls and checking the seed containers. The quiet was broken by Justin's singing and Ron's gentle humming stopped to register the song.

'Just hark at that blackbird, how can a simple little bird sing so divinely? What a voice?' His eyes searched for the source of the velvet notes.

He watched. He listened. His sharp brain could not compute the data collected by his eyes and ears. Mr Tolly's theatrical skills came to the fore, his movements in perfect sync with Justin's song. His body lengthened to reach a high note and Ron saw the missing feathers around his neck.

'I recognise that pigeon', he breathed, 'that's the pigeon that was caught behind the bay tree the other day.' He watched and listened.

'The poor little fellow must have damaged his throat and now he sings like a blackbird. He has returned to haunt me. Very likely, his flock has rejected him. What a tragedy, cast out for ever to sing alone. It would have been kinder to have killed him and put him in a pie.'

When the performance was over, Elvis called them away. Justin followed, but Mr Tolly remained, bowing to his former enemy.

Elvis went back for him. 'Come on, Mr Tolly, our work is done, back to the bridge.' One final bow and off to the nest he flew.

But Mr Tolly was not alone.

He greeted his family warmly, his old happy self again, all of his problems behind him. He had hardly settled on his beloved chicks when Mrs Tolly asked, 'and who are your friends?'

He looked around and there, on the crossbeam, perched a flock of lovelorn blackbird hens.

'Tell us a story, Dad,' said Crispin.

The 16.42 made its way to Chatham via Gravesend.

Pigeon Post

Kidnap

'Where's Alf? And where's Mrs Tolly?'

An urgent message had reached Mr Tolly whilst he foraged for food in Greenwich Park. On his return to the nest, he discovered Crispin – alone in the nest.

Crispin explained that Alf had tried to fly;

'He could fly down easily but then seemed to have difficulty flying up. And then an old man came along, put him in a box and walked away with him.'

'And where's Mrs Tolly?'

'She followed the man.'

Mr Tolly fed Crispin and comforted him. After what seemed an age Mrs Tolly returned. She caught her breath and recounted her story.

'I followed the old man to a bus stop. He took the bus and I hitched a ride until he alighted and then I followed him to his house. I watched from the roof and heard some cooing coming from a shed in the garden. I took a closer look and, through the wire, I could see, pigeons, dozens of pigeons trapped inside.'

'There, there, don't fret so Mrs Tolly.'

A crowd had gathered and there were mumblings, 'Mr Tolly will sort it out,' and 'nobody messes with Mr Tolly'.

Mr and Mrs Tolly touched beaks and Mr Tolly sensed that she was holding something back. Through the tears, she blurted, 'I think it's a pie factory. A pigeon pie factory.'

'Coo.'

Mr Tolly remained calm. 'Did you see Alf?'

'No, I looked everywhere.'

'Mrs Tolly – take me to the pie factory.'

They left Crispin in the safe care of the neighbours and flew as fast as their wings could carry them.

The pair alighted on the roof of the house and Mrs Tolly pointed to the pie factory.

'Wait here, I'm going to talk to those pigeons, they might have seen Alf.' He glided down and skidded to a halt on a plastic garden table level with the wire netting. Behind him stood another shed, a homemade ramshackle lean-to construction. It housed more pigeons. He peered into the enclosure searching frantically for Alf.

'Hi there. What's your name?' Asked a pigeon from behind the wire.

'Mr Tolly,' he responded with a polite bow. 'I feel driven to liberate you all, but first I must find a young chick, my son Alf, who has been kidnapped. Have you seen him?'

'No problem. Wait there a moment' said the incarcerated pigeon.

'Let me introduce myself,' the same bird joined him on the table. 'I'm Petroc, I live here. The wire netting is not to keep us in but to protect us racing pigeons from cats and foxes. We can come and go as we please. No problem.'

'Racing pigeons? What about Alf? He isn't a racing pigeon, he can't even fly, the pie man kidnapped him and I want him back!'

'Absolutely, no worries, I heard about the new recruit, Mr Noon picked him up from under a bridge at Greenwich. He had been abandoned and Mr Noon rescued him. He's safe, no worries'.

'Now listen Mr blooming *no worries*, I am worried, he wasn't abandoned, he was trying to fly and I want to see him now!'

'Call me Petroc, of course you can see him, absolutely, no problem but he's in our care now, we'll teach him to fly first.'

Mr Tolly flew to the roof to let Mrs Tolly know that at least Alf was alive and well. Petroc followed him.

'Wow, you're fast, we could use a pigeon like you in the team.'

'This is Petroc, he lives in the shed but says it's a team of racing pigeons and not a pie factory at all.'

'Super. We're very well fed, a balanced diet of corn and cereal, clean water, safe from predators. What more could a pigeon want?'

Mrs Tolly took a step forward – Petroc took a step back.

'I want my Alf back, that's what this pigeon wants, not a balanced diet, I want my Alf and I want him now.'

'I can do nothing, Mr Noon keeps the new recruits in the house for special training and assessment, then if they show promise, they're ringed and join the rest of us, first in the lean-to and then in the main shed, super. Good food, flea powder, why don't you come and have look? No obligation.'

'And what if they don't show promise? What then?' Mr Tolly interjected.

'Scleech.' A rat in the eaves below drew a claw across his scrawny throat. He had been eavesdropping.

'What?'

At the sound of the rat's *'scleech'* Petroc took off. 'Well, think over my proposition, must fly, have a nice day, super.' He hurried to the shed.

Mr Tolly talked into the roof tiles. 'What do you mean *'scleech'*? And who are you?'

'Scleech,' answered the rat, drawing the claw across his throat again. 'Twist and pull, dead quick, excuse the pun, then in the recycling bin with the leftovers from the takeaway. Name's Ed, by the way, I live here.'

Mrs Tolly formed the dreadful sound with her beak without uttering it, and she pulled her wing across her throat. She understood perfectly well the peril that threatened Alf.

'Mr Noon is an expert, he gets plenty of practice, for every ten new recruits he stretches the neck of about nine of them, *scleech*. How old is your Alf?'

'He can't even fly yet,' replied Mr Tolly into the tiles.

'Oh, he'll be OK for a while,' came the disembodied reassurance 'but you want to get him out of here before he becomes brainwashed.'

'What do you mean?'

'Mr Noon is crafty; he feeds them the best food, keeps 'em warm and cosy until they're completely dependent on him. He moves them to the lean-to for a month or so, they see the others flying to and fro, they get their bearings and feel comfortable in these surroundings. By the time they're moved to the main shed, he has 'em hooked. The pigeons have forgotten how to forage for food, they're free to fly away but always come back.'

'What about the racing?'

'He drives a whole basket of pigeons hundreds of miles away in the van and releases them.'

'So they escape.' Said Mrs Tolly.

'No, that's what's weird about it, they return. Mr Noon gets back first and registers each one as they arrive, noting the number on the leg ring. He breeds from the fast ones, some never return for some reason, and those who always come last, *scleech* – no good for racing, see, so *scleech*. "Can't waste food on slow coaches", I've heard him say often enough. You want to get young Alf out of here, and quickly.'

'But how can we help him escape? How can we reach him if he's in the house?'

'Well, I don't normally interfere, it's easy living, see, warm and dry, no cats and Mr Noon puts down food for me, well, rat poison to be more precise, but you get used to it. Tell you what, I'm feeling benevolent today, I'll see if I can find him, but it'll have to wait till it gets dark. Come back tomorrow at midday.'

Ed was a good-hearted rat, but years on a diet of rat poison had left its mark, bulging eyes and acres of bare wrinkly skin where fur used to grow. His tail was shorter than the average rat tail, he had lost that together with one ear in a fight with a cat. "But you should see the cat", he often remarked when recalling the altercation.

He was as good as his word, though, and at midnight he made his way to the large kitchen. Along one wall, where there would normally be cupboards, were shelves of bird cages of different shapes and sizes. Ed clambered amongst them until he saw a chick slumped alone on the floor of an old budgie cage.

'Pst, wake up. Are you Alf?' Alf shuffled towards Ed the rat.

'Shush, don't wake Russell, if he starts barking it'll wake Mr Noon.' Russell, a Yorkshire terrier, slept snuggly in a cat basket.

The clouds in the night sky shifted and, for a moment, Alf and Ed were illuminated by a shard of reflected moonlight; and each were taken aback by the other's appearance.

Ed told of his chat with Mr and Mrs Tolly and that an attempt to free him was being planned.

'How good is your flying?'

Alf explained that he was having trouble with direction, down was easy, but up, he conceded, was a little trickier.

'Yea, I have the same problem. That makes escaping just a tad more complicated than I originally imagined.' Ed tried the cage door, it opened easily, and he closed it again.

How was he to liberate a half-grown, half-feathered pigeon chick, who couldn't fly? He sat with his back to the cage surveying the kitchen. His bulging eyes noticed the cat flap in the door.

Mr Noon had processed the cat the same way as his underperforming birds when it ate one of his prize winning pigeons.

Ed scurried along the shelf, down a pipe and over the tiled floor to the kitchen door. Russell snored reassuringly. Ed gave the cat flap a push – then a pull, to no avail. He noticed a slide bolt and gave it a twist and a shove. Reluctantly, it shifted allowing the flap to open stiffly on the rusty hinges. He slid the bolt so that it just held the flap in position. He had no desire to struggle with it during the escape which was beginning to form in his head.

One terrier eye opened. Russell smelt the fresh air from outside. He maintained his regular breathing but his pulse raced. The dog was the perfect addition to his master's menagerie, a good ratter who didn't eat pigeons – an alternative cat. The second eye opened. Four legs tensed and took the weight of the taut body. Alf looked from one mammal to the other and sounded the alarm.

'Coo.'

The terrier's strong legs propelled him from the basket, shooting it away on the ceramic tiles. He sped towards the rat, focussing on the headlight eyes. Ed reached for the bolt and released it. Russell, teeth barred, snarling to the kill, straightened his front legs and skidded like Bambi on ice … Ed timed his side step to perfection, sending the dog yapping through the cat flap into the cold night air.

'About time I wasn't here. See you tomorrow, Alf.' He slid the bolt, locking the cat flap and silently left the scene of the crime.

The light went on, Mr Noon stormed across the kitchen, unlocked the door and let the yapping dog in.

'How on earth did you get out there?'

The sleepy old man settled the little dog in the basket. He inspected the kitchen for signs of a break-in and eventually turned the light off and slowly climbed the stairs.

'I smell a rat,' he murmured as he pulled the quilt over.

Escape

Mr Noon entered the kitchen ready to start his morning routine, kettle on, toast in, it was the same every morning. He pushed the door open and hooked it back against the outside wall. A chill autumn breeze rushed into the kitchen, replacing the stale animal air. The dog stretched his legs and investigated his usual places.

'What was all that last night? How on earth did you get out here? I need my sleep. Was it that rat?' He paused as if expecting an answer.

'I'm going to get that rat, mark my words, that rat is as good as dead.'

He checked the birds in the shed and in the lean-to, giving them food and water. Assured that all was well, man and dog returned to the warmth of the kitchen.

'Brrr, it's cold out there.' He rubbed his hands together and closed the door. On the way to the toaster, he stopped to look through the bars at Alf.

'I don't quite see you invigorating my blood stock.'

Ed's bulbous eyes were watching the morning routine through a gap in the ceiling boards, and he made mental rat notes along the way.

The old man sat with a cup of tea and a piece of toast, scanning the kitchen to see how Russell might have escaped. He rose from the table, toast in hand, and checked the windows; they were secure and the door had been locked. His glance fell to the cat flap and he gave it a closer examination, unbolted it, opened and closed it, then pushed the bolt firmly into the locked position. Convinced that the episode would remain a mystery, he said 'come on, Houdini, it's time for your morning walk.'

Man and bouncing, barking dog left by the front door.

Ed made his way to the kitchen and immediately tried the cat flap. Mr Noon had jammed it into the locked position, Ed couldn't budge it.

At midday, three pigeons landed on the apex of the roof, Mr and Mrs Tolly had invited Elvis along. Mercedes the sparrow hawk watched from a nearby tree.

Mr Tolly talked into the roof tiles.

'Ed, are you there?'

'No.'

'Who are you then?'

'It's me, Ed.'

'I thought you said you weren't there.'

'I'm not.'

Elvis interrupted. 'Enough of this nonsense. Can you help Alf escape or can't you?'

'No, go away, I can't help, no one can, it's hopeless, forget him.'

'You must help, it's my Alf,' pleaded Mrs Tolly.

Ed recounted his nocturnal activities – about the cage door being easy, but the windows and door were locked and now the cat flap was jammed.

'Alf can't fly, that's the problem. If he could fly, it would be a doddle, I could open the cage, and when Mr Noon hooks the door back while he feeds the birds, Alf could scarper. But he can't fly, so forget him, that's my advice.'

Elvis said, 'what if he was carried out through the open door?'

Ed looked up to the tiles, 'yea, that's a great idea, "jump on my back Alf, *hi-yo Silver,"* perhaps a little saddle.'

'Very funny', said Elvis, 'what if a bird grabbed him and flew him out through the door.'

'A bird? What sort of bird?'

'A sparrow hawk.'

'A sparrow hawk?' laughed Ed, 'a sparrow hawk in that kitchen? With all those flighty pigeons? It would be mayhem.'

'Mayhem is underrated', said Elvis. 'You say the old man leaves the kitchen door open, when does he do that?

'Shortly after dawn, as the light comes up.'

'This is the plan.' He signalled to Mercedes and she swooped elegantly to join them on the roof.

'Ed, meet Mercedes, she'll make the snatch.'

'Pleased to meet you, Mercedes,' said Ed. Elvis proceeded to outline his plan.

'Ed, your task is to help Alf out of the cage. Is there a place where he can be picked up?'

'Yes, on the shelf by the cage.' Ed described the kitchen. He would be ready with Alf. Mercedes explained how she wanted Alf positioned.

'On his back with his feet in the air, as near to the edge as possible. That will give me optimal wing clearance. Tell Alf I'll grab his feet and carry him off through the open door. I'll be less tempted to eat him in that position.'

Mrs Tolly gulped a pigeon gulp.

'Is that clear, Ed?' asked Mercedes.

'What if Mr Noon sees you flying in through the door? It's only a small yard. You can see that if you look down, he could quickly close the door, trapping you inside.' That set them thinking and Elvis checked the yard, noting the distance between the two sheds and the kitchen door.

'You have a point there, Ed.'

'Mrs Tolly and I could easily create a diversion on the table by the shed?'

'What kind of diversion?' asked Elvis.

'There's an inmate called Petroc, he tried to smooth-talk me into joining the racing team, thought me a very fast flyer, which of course is true ...'

'Keep to the point.'

'If Mrs Tolly and I engage him in conversation, the old man would certainly take notice, we know he's keen to expand his team of athletically gifted birds. It would also create calm, you know how we pigeons react to the sight of a sparrow hawk. No offence, Mercedes,' he said, shifting a little.

'None taken, one cannot tinker with the natural order of the food chain. No offence, Mr Tolly.' He took another step away.

Agreed on the plan of action for the next morning, they all left, apart from Elvis. The dawn raid played through his head – Ed the rat preparing Alf – Alf on his back – Mr and Mrs Tolly on the table outside – Mercedes swooping in for the grab.

'And me. What will my role be?'

Mayhem

Mr and Mrs Tolly alighted on the plastic table. He whispered 'have courage. We stand our ground. If the dog barks, or if the old man approaches, we don't take flight. This is for Alf.'

The door opened and Russell rushed out yapping and sniffing around. Mr Noon hooked the door back and returned to the boiling kettle and toaster.

Ed observed through the crack.

The smell of toast wafted into the still autumn air and the old man pushed his nose against Alf's cage.

'The recycling bin is collected tomorrow.' The dog rushed in, jumping up for some toast.

'Hi.' The potential recruits were joined on the table by Petroc. Mr Tolly moved so that he could see into the kitchen and Petroc could not.

'Super to see you both.'

'Come on dog, let's attend to our morning chores.' Mr Noon stopped just outside the door, he straightened his back and stretched his arms wide, inhaling the fresh air deeply into his lungs.

'Hello. What have we here?' He approached slowly, talking gently to the birds on the table. 'I don't think we've been introduced.'

Ed scuttled into the kitchen, made his way to the cage and opened the door. 'Come on, young Alf, flying time.' He clambered into the cage and pushed the chick to the opening. Alf landed with a thump on the shelf.

'Now, on your back as I explained last night. That's it, as close to the edge as possible. Try not to panic, the sparrow hawk is coming to rescue you, not eat you.' Alf lay on his back, feet in the air, his little heart pounding.

'Be brave, be brave.' He repeated the mantra taught to him by the rat.

'Three, two, one, go.' Elvis and Mercedes glided towards the door like acrobats on a trapeze.

'Good work, Petroc' whispered the old man. He was so engaged in this little operation that he saw nothing of the invasion of his kitchen. He reached underneath to a butterfly net which hung ready for such an opportunity as this.

The rescuers swept into the kitchen. Alf panicked, corrected his position and bolted between two cages mumbling 'be brave, be brave.'

Mercedes settled on a high shelf and waited motionlessly. Ed had Alf by the feet and was dragging him back to the planned position.

'There, there, it's alright, you'll be safe soon. This is goodbye my little friend, but come back when you have learned how to fly. I'll miss you.'

While Ed dragged Alf to the brink, Elvis flitted from cage to cage, opening the doors one by one.

'Wait for the signal to fly, then we all fly together to freedom.'

Mr Noon held Mr Tolly and stroked him on the beak. 'You might be a little stout for racing, but a few months on a strict diet might do the trick.' The net trapped Mrs Tolly on the table.

Most of the cage doors were open. Elvis tugged franticly on the last one.

Ed had Alf near the edge, a firm grip on each leg. He glanced towards the door.

'He's coming back!'

'Hang on Ed', shouted Mercedes, 'hang on tight.' She dived and grabbed Ed's not so long rat tail firmly in her talons as it dangled over the edge. She dipped precariously under the weight as she dragged them both from the shelf.

'GO – FLY TO FREEDOM' shouted Elvis.

Mercedes, Ed and Alf led the way – passing Mr Noon at about knee height, almost colliding with him.

'What the blue blazes ...?'

A rush of wind accompanied the sound of pigeons in flight. Elvis was the last to leave.

'Meet me in the deer enclosure at Greenwich Park', he called.

'I'm flying, I'm flying' shouted Alf.

'You will be if I let go' said Ed.

'So will you if I let go,' added Mercedes silencing them both.

Mr Noon, with Mr Tolly firmly in his grasp, stood mouth agape watching his flock disappearing into the distance. The dog ran in circles barking and Mrs Tolly struggled hopelessly under the net.

Focusing on the old man, Elvis circled once, took aim and dived towards the upturned face, closer – closer, he rotated his wings, slowed – pulled his undercarriage forward and – *squidge* – *splat*.

Mr Noon really should have kept his mouth closed. It was a direct hit. He released his grip on Mr Tolly who flew into the air.

'Aaaah ...' spluttered Mr Noon, blinded.

'Quick', called Elvis. Elvis and Mr Tolly took hold of the rim of the butterfly net and lifted it together, and Mrs Tolly was free.

From a branch high in a tree, the three reflected on the scene in the garden, the yapping dog and Mr Noon spluttering and blindly bumping into things.

'A good mornings work,' said Elvis 'Mrs Tolly, why don't you check out Alf at the park and how about you, Mr Tolly, flying back to the bridge to inform Crispin that his brother has been rescued. I have some unfinished business here.'

Detoxification

The flock of liberated pigeons grazed peacefully in the deer enclosure. Ed the rat had taken on the task of teaching Alf to fly.

'That's it, flap your wings. No, no, no, you have to run fast. It would help if you had some feathers,' he reflected. 'I must say I've never seen a bald bird fly.'

Mrs Tolly spotted Alf amongst the others and flew down for a happy reunion.

'Look Mum, Ed's is teaching me to fly.' She stepped aside to let the lessons continue.

High in a towering oak, the owl brothers Merlin and Bouncer watched, pondering the rat's qualification as a flying instructor.

'He'll never get off the ground with so few feathers' said Merlin.

'You're right', agreed his brother, 'a couple more weeks before he's ready.'

Ed was running ahead, upright on his hind legs and flapping his front ones like wings when he slowed to a crawl, stumbled and fell flat on his face. He lay twitching and foaming at the mouth.'

'What's the matter?' Alf rushed to his aid.

'Ed is dead. Quick – help!'

The flock of pigeons came to see. They gathered around. The twitching stopped; Ed lay still on his side. The rat's swollen eyes were closed, the thin-veined lids barely adequate.

'He moved' said one of the birds.

'Wake up, Ed; you have to teach me how to fly.'

One eye opened, 'poison', moaned the prostrate creature.

'He's been poisoned.'

'Rat poison', croaked Ed.

'He has been fed rat poison.'

'No, I need some poison,' Ed was coming round. 'I need some rat poison, and quick.'

They sat him up and gave him some water from a dried out conker shell. Ed was shaking and sweating, he told the flock how he started on rat poison which Mr Noon had placed at a spot where he knew the rat would find it.

'It made me ill at first but it was so delicious I just kept on eating it. My eyes began to swell and my fur fell out,' he bemoaned. 'I haven't always looked like this, you know.'

A squirrel called Egmont had been listening. 'I know where to find rat poison. I can fetch some if you like.'

'No, it'll kill him', said Alf.

'Better call a quack then', said Egmont. 'I know a good one. I'll go find him.'

A large handsomely marked mallard landed heavily in the deer enclosure. He introduced himself as Doctor Henry and proclaimed that if Ed continued to eat rat poison as a staple diet, it would certainly kill him, but that if he stopped suddenly that could also kill him or at least be most unpleasant.

'You must switch to a diet of oats from the deer trough, nuts and fruit from the park and bread that the humans bring for us ducks. The transition must be gradual, reducing the rat poison to nil over as short a period as possible, three weeks would be sensible. The squirrel who came for me is fetching the rat poison now and I will show you how much to take.'

While this drama unfolded, Mr Tolly delivered his own dramatic account of Alf's rescue to Crispin and a cluster of neighbours at the bridge.

***

Elvis surveyed the pigeon fancier's small suburban garden and the sheds which housed the remaining birds. Mr Noon was nowhere to be seen.

Elvis had prepared some things to say to Petroc about freedom, about the daily challenge for survival which the racing pigeons had exchanged for artificial food, vitamin supplements and flea powder. He wanted to remind these pigeons, who were prisoners by choice, of the responsibility of all free birds and animals to exercise that liberty out of respect to those less fortunate creatures who were born into captivity and who had no choice. But the fine words would have to wait – the rescue was not yet complete. His concern was for the partially brainwashed pigeons in the lean-to. Those in the main shed were beyond help, but hope remained for the lean-to residents.

Elvis's deliberations were interrupted when Mr Noon burst into the yard from the kitchen. His face was red from a combination of scrubbing and rage. He was mumbling to himself;

'That's it. It's over. No more pigeons, I'm selling them all.' He went to the shed.

'I should get a tidy sum for you lot.' He set the entrance so that the birds could enter but not leave, then stepped across the yard to the lean-to, 'and as for you worthless lot, *scleech*,' he drew a finger across his throat, 'tonight, when it's dark, ready for the recycling bin'. He went back into the house.

Elvis flew down to the table and spoke through the wire netting.

'So, Petroc, you are trapped, what are your plans now?'

'We'll simply be sold on to another pigeon fancier and retrained, life goes on.'

'And what about those in the lean-to? Asked Elvis pointing with his wing. 'Life goes on you say ... but not for them, you heard the old man.'

'Most unfortunate, I must say. But that's Mr Noon's decision. Nothing to do with me'.

'We must release them before nightfall or they'll die. D'you know how to open the door?'

Petroc returned to the feeder. Elvis flew across the yard to the lean-to. The structure was clearly homemade, cobbled together with odd bits of timber, the door was an old internal one with the panels knocked out and fine wire stapled over. He flew to the fence and viewed it from there. He noticed that it was wide at the top and narrow at the bottom 'for the rain to fall away, I suppose,' thought Elvis, 'clever, these humans.'

He flew back for a closer look and, on landing on the roof, sensed a slight movement. He walked to where the roof joined the wall, there was a narrow gap. He inspected the gap, and as he did, a bird landed behind him, the gap widened ... it was Petroc.

'Petroc? How did you escape from the shed? The old man fixed the exit.'

'I'm a clever bird. But not a very nice bird. And I don't expect you ever to like me, but let me help you save these poor condemned pigeons.'

'Take off and land again.'

Petroc obeyed. Elvis watched the gap. 'Again, land near the edge.' The whole structure was loose, it moved away from the wall as Petroc landed, only slightly, but it moved. Elvis flew to the fence, then to the tree and finally to the table. He surveyed the structure from all angles. Only then did he know how to spring the birds.

'Can you help the pigeons escape from the main shed?'

'Yes, of course, no problem.'

'Do it now, I want them all on the roof here.'

Petroc landed on the plastic garden table and began to mobilise the racing pigeons. Elvis spoke to the lean-to occupants, their cooperation was critical.

'On the perch here, this one, all of you.' He gestured to the perch furthest from the wall. One by one the racers joined Elvis on the sloping roof. Their weight alone was insufficient.

'Jump and land again.' Elvis kept his eye on the gap.

'Again, together this time,' the gap widened slightly then closed again.

'And you birds inside on the perch – listen to my instructions. I want you to hover and drop together on my count – up two three and drop – up two three, drop – up two three, drop.'

The landings became increasingly coordinated and the gap widened more and returned less each time. Elvis could see the screws and the fixing plugs coming away from their holes. The sixth landing was perfect, as was the seventh. It was at that moment they heard Russell barking from the kitchen. There was almost enough space for a pigeon to squeeze through. The eighth landing was accompanied by a creaking noise. Through the kitchen window, Elvis saw Mr Noon approaching – reaching for the door handle. On the ninth landing Elvis jumped, too, and the lean-to came completely away from the wall and fell across the door preventing it from opening.

There followed a jubilant explosion of flight.

The lean-to – leaned no more.

'To the park' called Elvis.

*

Ed wolfed down his dose of rat poison greedily, 'that's not very much' he said looking at the empty conker shell.

'Three times a day for week, twice a day for the second week and once a day for the third week. And don't let him know your source Egmont, he may try to follow you.' Dr Henry warned.

*

Ed's fur grew back and his eyes gradually became proportionate with his body. Alf's feathers grew, too, and his airworthiness improved so that he was soon looping the loop with his brother Crispin.

Ed the rat and his pals Alf and Crispin lived together in an abandoned nest box in Greenwich Park. Ed told stories from his time living at Mr Noon's house and, in return, Alf and Crispin retold some of Mr Tolly's tales.

The owl brothers, Bouncer and Merlin observed these strange happenings, unaware that Mr Tolly was soon to play a significant role in a momentous adventure that could potentially change the whole relationship between the animal kingdom and humans.

The Royal Egg

Discovery

The doorbell rang and Helen let Uncle Bob in.

'Come on through, Dad's in the garden with the plant.'

'That's it,' Andy pointed to a lone plant in the middle of the raised bed. It stood about a foot tall, had a dozen or so largish leaves and a conker crowned the main stem – or certainly a fruit that resembled a conker.

'Well, Bob, what do you think it is? I can't find anything like it in my gardening books.'

Helen and her dad watched Bob expectantly. He rubbed his chin. 'It looks like a horse chestnut or some kind of prickly pear.' He squatted on his haunches for a closer look.

The fruit certainly resembled a conker, but it was more egg shaped, and it seemed to grow on its end at the main stem of a hybrid squash plant.

'You're pulling my leg,' said Bob. 'You've stuck a conker on a courgette plant with the help of a cocktail stick.' He looked closer, pushing his glasses up onto his forehead and dipping lower to locate the join. There was no join, nor was it a conker, the prickles were too far apart.

'Mm, I'll have to look it up in my "Encyclopaedia of Exotic Plants". When did you discover it?'

'That's what's so strange. I cleared that bed yesterday, which means that is has grown to that size overnight.'

'You need new glasses', said Helen running into the house. 'I'm going to help Mum put lunch on the table. See you in a bit.'

The two brothers did a tour of the garden in the early autumn light.

*

But Helen's dad hadn't been the first to discover the strange plant. A highly agitated Mr Tolly found himself on the high branches of one of the oldest oak trees in Greenwich Park. He was about to attempt the impossible – an audience with a very important bird – Old Owl.

Old Owl was by far the oldest bird for miles around. She was so old that she hardly flew at all, and when she did, the take-off and landing had to be carefully choreographed with the help of other owls.

The lowly pigeon and the dignified matriarch of Greenwich Park were about to meet; Mr Tolly and Old Owl.

'I've come to see Old Owl,' said Mr Tolly to the owl guarding the nest, which was a large hole in the trunk near the top of the tree. A broad branch led straight to the opening for easy access when she performed one of her spectacular landings.

'It's the middle of the day, Old Owl is asleep – come back later,' said Bouncer.

'No it has to be now. It's really important … I've been sent,' insisted Mr Tolly who was behaving strangely and seemed to be driven by some external force.

'And who sent you, may I ask?'

'I don't know exactly, I just know that it's of utmost importance that I speak with Old Owl.'

'If you haven't an appointment – and you haven't – you can't see her, now scoot!', said the big bird taking a step towards him.

'Old Owl,' shouted Mr Tolly, 'I must see you.' Bouncer approached and lunged with his beak. Mr Tolly took off, dodged past him and dived through the opening.

With a 'thump' he hit a wall of soft downy feathers.

'What on earth?' blinked Old Owl. 'What's happening? Bouncer, I am being attacked.'

'It was the plant that sent me, there were vibrations, and the plant told me to fetch you.'

'I'll soon have him out, Old Owl. Come 'er lunch.' Bouncer approached, Mr Tolly ran behind Old Owl, tripped up in the dark and landed in a smelly pile of feathers and desiccated owl poo.

'No wait, leave us Bouncer, I'll call if I need you.' She focused on the intruder. 'You can come out now, whoever you are. Explain yourself.'

Mr Tolly tried to speak, spat out some feathers and tripped over again. Old Owl had moved to block the exit – and blank out the light. She could see him but he could not see her.

'You are a pigeon!' she declared, 'a common town pigeon'.

'It wasn't me' he tried to say, coughing up another feather. Old Owl shifted to let a chink of light in.

'It certainly was you. You're the only one here.'

'Let me explain.'

'Please do.'

He began. 'You see, it wasn't me. I was in a garden, grazing when the ground started to vibrate and a voice in my head, not my ears, you understand, a haunting voice said "Old Owl, Old Owl, tell her of me, she will know what to do". It wasn't a language, not bird nor human, nor animal and it was coming from the plant, this strange plant. I was drawn towards it, as if some power was pulling me. Then the voice again, even more compelling "go now, fly, fly. The time is soon." At first I thought I'd eaten something that didn't agree with ...'

'Keep to the point.' She had moved towards him, her face close to his, he felt her warm breath.

'Mm', thought Mr Tolly, 'a common town pigeon, eh?'

The owl turned to the opening and snapped, 'Bouncer, fetch Merlin and Judy as fast as you can.' She turned to Mr Tolly.

'What's your name pigeon?'

'Mr Tolly, at your service, ma'am.'

'Well get on with it – or I'll eat you.'

'OK, OK' he said. *'Eat me, my foot, she won't make a snack out of me.'* He thought. He continued slowly.

'The plant stood all alone in a raised bed; it had nine or ten leaves.'

'Ten', she said 'carry on.'

On top of the main stalk was a conker or what looked like a conker.'

Old Owl moved her face a little and stared at him thoughtfully.

'Who knows about this? Have you told any other birds or animals?'

'No, I came straight here. Everything in my mind was blanked out, I came straight to you as fast I could and if it hadn't been for muscles out there, I'd have reached you sooner, not that I was scared, mind you, I ...'

'Shush. Could you find the place again?'

'Yes.'

'Stay there and be quiet whilst I think.' She paced back and forth.

Mr Tolly was feeling mildly satisfied. 'This will make a great story for the new clutch of chicks next spring,' he thought. Whilst Old Owl paced to and fro, Mr Tolly gazed about the cavernous nest, comparing it to the simple collection of twigs that he and Mrs Tolly called home. He tried to interpret Old Owl's rambling utterances, 'the tenth ... a hundred years ... a thousand years ... outside the park ... the Chosen One ... kill the messenger ...'.

'*Kill the messenger*?' Mr Tolly began to think that now might be the appropriate time to be frightened.

'Well, thank you for your kind hospitality, I think I had better be going.'

'Oh Mr Tolly, you are going nowhere. I need you.'

At the sound of birds talking outside, Old Owl left to meet Merlin and Judy and, looking over her shoulder (owls are good at this), she said, 'don't think of leaving, I have hungry hawks waiting outside.'

Mr Tolly was inside the nest alone. 'I'm done for this time' he thought, '*kill the messenger*' echoed in his ears.

'Why me? Why couldn't that stupid plant have chosen some other bird?' He settled down to enjoy some sad thoughts.

Bouncer blocked the entrance. Sometimes he was looking in and sometimes he was looking out. Mr Tolly's thoughts grew sadder.

Old Owl met with Bouncer's brother, Merlin, and Judy – a crow of great intellect and knowledge. Merlin and Judy, under the direction of Old Owl and with the assistance of Bouncer, had ahead of them a task – a task so monumental that its successful completion could potentially change the established order of the world. Failure would result in a delay of a hundred years.

The Secret of the Royal Egg

The secret of the Royal Egg had passed through generations of owls, exclusively owls, but now the secret would be shared with Judy, a crow.

They perched outside on the landing branch, Judy was sworn to secrecy and Old Owl began:

'Let me outline what's at stake'. She spoke earnestly, her old eyes burning passionately.

'Since the beginning of time, there has been inequality and misunderstanding between the human race and the animal kingdom. A thousand years ago, an opportunity to rectify this manifested itself when the first Royal Egg was found in Greenwich Park. The egg contained a manuscript … a manuscript that could be read by humans, animals and birds. Some monks discovered a group of village children reading it together with birds and animals. They declared it witchcraft, seized the document and punished the children. The monks were confused and frightened; few were able to read in those days and certainly not children. However, before the manuscript was burned, an owl managed to read and memorise part of it. On the last page, it was written that the next Royal Egg would appear in a hundred years' time and that the owls of Greenwich Park had to be ready for it.

That owl, and ancestor, kept the story alive by ensuring that, as each year passed, it was counted by carving a scar in the bark of a young oak sapling here in Greenwich Park. Owls learn about the Royal Egg when they are ten years old. The 'Annual Marking and Remembering Ceremony' is attended by the owls of Greenwich Park in order to keep the memory alive.'

Merlin interjected, 'that oak tree is known as "Queen Elizabeth's Oak", it died recently and a new one has been planted nearby.'

Old Owl continued, 'that was a thousand years ago and the tenth Royal Egg is here now and it's our duty to ensure its safety.'

'Will it mean that animals and humans will be able to speak to each other?' Asked Judy.

'That happens already, although it's rare and generally it's children who have the ability. It's thought to be temporary and any memory of the event is erased – any recall being explained as a dream.' She paused philosophically. 'You see, for some inexplicable reason, human beings are convinced that they are the superior species,' the others chuckled at this absurd notion.

'It's a most serious misjudgement on their part; the entire animal kingdom is embarrassed by their behaviour towards each other and us birds and animals.'

'They can't even fly without machines,' laughed Merlin.

'Humans are very intelligent, though,' added Bouncer.'

'Quite right, they are intelligent,' agreed Old Owl, 'but they so often use that gift wrongly, groups conduct wars against other groups, just because they're different. Intelligence is a great asset, but shouldn't be confused with wisdom.

It is thought that each Royal Egg has contributed in some way to convince humans that they should reassess their relationship with the animal kingdom and the planet we share.'

'But what is going to hatch from the Royal Egg?' asked Judy.

'No one knows. We have to be ready for every eventuality – bird, animal, plant, seed, formulae, written instructions, a book – anything at all. We have to be prepared to deal with it, whatever form it takes. Our task is to ensure that it moves on to the next stage.'

'The next stage?'

'Yes, and we don't know what that will be until it hatches. The most challenging will be a live creature. If it is, we have to keep it alive and move it to an environment where it will thrive. The fruit of this Royal Egg will probably be with us for a short time only. It's odd that our Royal Egg has not been found within the walls of Greenwich Park – most strange indeed.

But the time for talking is over … we must act … that pigeon in there has found the Royal Egg and we have to move fast.

The spirit of the Royal Egg has communicated to us through Mr Tolly. Time is critical, the egg develops rapidly, days rather than weeks or months. Nine Royal Eggs, a thousand years and now the tenth – this is our calling – this is our moment. Top of the agenda is to locate the Royal Egg and we need Mr Tolly for that.

This is the plan: Judy, Bouncer and Merlin fly with this plump pigeon to the place of the Royal Egg. Check if there's enough space in the garden for me to land, remember I need a clear approach and a long runway to take off again. Once we have located the garden 'kill the messenger' … that's the procedure, he is of no further use to us. Fetch Mr Tolly.

If the owls had their 'Secret of the Royal Egg', Mr Tolly had his secret, too: the secret of very keen pigeon ears. He was ready for them, and was going nowhere until he had a guarantee of survival in his current form, i.e. one healthy, whole pigeon.

Bouncer moved aside and Judy went to fetch him. She peered into the dark.

Mr Tolly stood defiant in the middle of the floor, his chest thrust forward and his wing pointing to the crow.

'Now … and if … just to say … I am … because … indeed … and no and not.' Mr Tolly, in his nervous state had lost the power of cohesive speech.

'Just one moment, Mr Tolly' said Judy, she recognised him. His upright poise had exposed the scar on his neck where he had been trapped.

She left and turned to Old Owl.

'That stopped her in her tracks,' mumbled Mr Tolly.

'What's up' said Old Owl, 'has he escaped?'

'No he hasn't escaped, but do you know who he is?'

'He's some common feral pigeon called Mr Tolly. Is there something else I should know?'

'This is no ordinary pigeon, he has special powers, he sings like a blackbird,' said Judy.

'Oh, I've heard of this singing pigeon – is this one and the same bird? That makes a significant difference. It means that our Mr Tolly must be the Chosen One.

'The Chosen One?'

'Yes, which is most unusual, the Chosen One is normally a human, most often a human child. That shines a different light on the matter. Protect him at all costs; ensure no harm comes to a single Tolly feather. Now go – time is everything.'

'You were saying?' said Judy to Mr Tolly.

'Was I? Oh yes, indeed I was saying, let us tarry not ... time and tide wait for no pigeon ... many mickle maks a ... something ... onward and upward ... follow me to the garden.'

Retrieval

Old Owl watched the four birds disappear through the tree tops of Greenwich. She pulled herself to her full height, stretched her wings and moved them slowly through their full range. Her muscles were weak and her body heavy, but her brain was as sharp as her beak.

'I will have to keep an eye on Mr Tolly, he has exceptionally good hearing.'

This was her moment, all her life, the past hundred years, the past ten centuries shone a penetrating flood of light on the next few hours.

*

'Now, where's that blessed conker plant?' Mr Tolly flew from garden to garden, landing on the fences in his search for the plant.

'All these gardens look the same. It must be the next street,' he shouted to Judy, who followed one fence behind. She looked to Merlin and Bouncer, who sat together observing from the high branch of a tree.

'I thought pigeons possessed special navigational skills which set them apart from other birds,' said Bouncer.

'Not this one. Although he apparently sings like a blackbird.'

'Which is useful considering the rarity of blackbirds in this neighbourhood.'

Then Mr Tolly saw it. He landed in the garden just to make certain, then flew up to the fence and beckoned to Judy.

They walked reverently towards the strange plant.

'It has grown,' said Mr Tolly.

It had. Within a few hours, the conker fruit had expanded and was now the size of a coconut. The stem had thickened and grown from one foot to one yard.

Bouncer and Merlin joined them on the little lawn and they, too, stood in awe of the plant.

Judy asked their opinion on the landing possibilities for Old Owl. They weighed up the situation while Mr Tolly took a moment to graze the lawn.

'It's too small,' said Merlin. 'The side fences are too high and too close together. The trees at that end and the house at the other makes it much too enclosed.'

'You're right, Merlin, the garden isn't long enough.'

'What do you think – Chosen One?'

Mr Tolly carried on grazing.

'Do you think Old Owl could land and take off in this small space Chosen One?' Judy asked trying to catch his eye.

'Who? What? Me?' He looked behind him and then at Judy again. 'What land in this garden? Old Owl? Yes land and take off again. That shouldn't be a problem.' He registered their sceptical glances and so flew to one fence and then the other, looking expertly this way and that. Then to the roof and did the same thing.

'Yup, that'll be fine', he confirmed, landing again on the lawn.

'I disagree, she isn't fit enough and she's too heavy.'

'Don't worry, Merlin. This is a very special occasion, and remember I'll be here,' nodded the Chosen One reassuringly.

'Yes,' said Merlin, 'that's what worries me. I'm going to the park and will brief Old Owl on our progress.' He beat his wings and lifted off across the gardens towards the park.

*

After lunch, Uncle Bob had left, Dad was snoozing in the armchair and Mum was washing her hair. Helen looked from her bedroom window.

'Dad, there's an owl in the garden and it's broad daylight.'

'Yes dear, that's nice.'

'It's talking with a crow and a fat pigeon.'

'Mm, good.'

*

Old Owl was insistent. Merlin had never seen her like this. 'I must be there to direct the operation.'

'Are you sure you want to risk it?'

'The risk is greater if I stay away. Any risk to my personal wellbeing is insignificant compared to the safety of the Royal Egg. I've waited all my life for this moment and the Chosen One says it will be alright, so stop fussing and take me to the garden.'

'OK, but don't say I didn't warn you.'

Both owls launched together, wings spread. An absence of thermals in the sheltered park caused Old Owl to lose height rapidly. Merlin positioned his powerful young body under hers and shared the weight. Within a few wing beats the timing synchronised. They gained height and he reduced the uplift until Old Owl flew independently. Merlin led the way and the older bird followed.

*

'Mum, another owl has just crash landed in the garden. What's going on?'

Mum was still in the bathroom. *'Three little maids from school are we ... la la ... all unwary* ... what was that, dear?'

*

'Blimey, I'm glad she didn't land on me. I'm supposedly the precious Chosen One,' thought Mr Tolly.

Old Owl was helped to her feet by Judy and Merlin.

'Where is it?'

They turned in silence and gazed at the plant. Old Owl took a step closer and stared at the sturdy bearer of the Royal Egg.

*

Helen had by now given up relaying bulletins to her parents and knelt on a chair to watch the spectacle from the window. One owl in the tree, two owls, a shiny crow and a plump pigeon on the lawn and they seemed very interested in the funny conker plant.

'That conker isn't a conker ... it's the size of a rugby ball. It's going to explode if it grows any bigger.'

*

'See the stalk is beginning to bend. When it reaches close to the ground that's when we take it,' said Old Owl.

'When you say "take it", what exactly do you mean?' said Judy. 'Take it where and how?'

'Take it to the park, to the nest, and how, that's why you are all here. We're the best bird brains to be found anywhere – oh, and Mr Tolly, the Chosen One.'

'What's in the egg?' asked Mr Tolly.

'That's the mystery. We don't know and we won't know until it hatches. But the question is – how do we carry it back to the nest?'

Carrier Owl

The kitchen door opened into the garden and Helen approached.

The ground vibrated as before and, in each of their heads, the birds heard:

'Trust Helen, speak, and she will understand.'

'Hello, who are you and what are you doing?'

Mr Tolly bowed and said, 'hello Helen we have to transport this Royal Egg to Greenwich Park. It's very urgent.'

'I can understand you. You know my name! Can you understand me?'

'Yes we can,' said Old Owl. 'The plant told us that you're to be trusted. Which means you're the Chosen One and that you're to help us.'

'Usurped', gulped Mr Tolly.

'Talking plants? Talking birds? But if you want to get that thing to Greenwich Park, I'll ask my dad and he'll drive it. I'm sure he would.'

Judy strutted forward. 'That's a good idea Helen, tell your dad that you're in conversation with two owls, a crow and a pigeon in the garden and that you'd like him to drive an enchanted egg to Greenwich Park, climb to the top of one of the highest oak trees in the park and deliver it to an owl's nest.'

'What you're saying is "leave my dad out of this".'

'And your mum, grown up humans tend complicate matters rather than help.'

Mr Tolly glanced at the Royal Egg. 'Look, all this talking and the Royal Egg is drooping.'

'We need a crane' said Merlin.

'Nobody here can operate a crane, and anyway, it can't be that heavy.'

'Not that sort of crane' said Merlin 'I meant the bird.'

Helen laughed. 'I think you mean a stork.'

'No time. Look at the Royal Egg, it's ready', said Old Owl. She hooted and Bouncer came down with a rush of wind. Bouncer could you carry the Royal Egg back to the nest?'

Bouncer approached the Royal Egg and wriggled underneath so that the egg balanced between his wings. He flexed his legs.

'Mm, the weight isn't a problem, but it won't stay there for long if I fly.'

'Carry it in your talons,' said Helen.

Bouncer slipped from under the Royal Egg and looked shyly at her. 'My talons are not big enough to go around it and, even if they were, the egg would be crushed under my grip.'

'No, not like that', she turned and ran into the house. She was back in a flash with her mum's canvas shopping bag.

'Carry it in this.'

'That could work.' Bouncer took the empty bag by the handles and flew up and around with it.

'That *will* work,' he announced on landing.

They went forward to the plant and Helen helped manoeuvre the Royal Egg into the shopping bag.

'It's time.' Old Owl looked at each of them one by one, drinking in the moment. She gripped the stalk in her beak and with one clean bite separated the Royal Egg from its host plant.

It was Bouncer who uncharacteristically directed flight operations.

'When I arrive at the nest, there has to be a bird inside to receive the Royal Egg – that will be you, Judy. Merlin – be ready to ease it forward through the opening while I hover over the entrance. Fly now and take up your positions. Mr Tolly stay close to me, I may need you.

Old Owl, wait for us here in the garden, we'll be back to help you into the air so that you can return to your nest and the Royal Egg.'

Helen, Mr Tolly and Old Owl moved aside to give Bouncer room for his vertical take-off.

He spread his enormous wings and began beating, dust and leaves swirling in the draft. Talons, vicelike, gripped the handles and took the weight, the creases in the bag smoothed and daylight appeared between the shopping bag and the ground. Wing tips met above and below, the lift was complete, Bouncer strained to gain height under the heavy load.

They watched enthralled as the owl and the Royal Egg disappeared over the rooftops.

'Aren't you supposed to be with him, Mr Tolly?'

'Ah yes, of course, better hurry along.'

He quickly caught up and could see the strain on Bouncer's face. He positioned himself under the egg and took some of the weight.

'Every little helps,' he shouted.

'Well done.'

Mr Tolly pushed up against the hard vegetable shell, through the bag he felt a softening and then a warmth emanating from the fruit of the egg.

'I think it has hatched,' he shouted.

Bouncer's huge heart swelled with pride and the blood coursed faster through his veins.

'I said, I think a chick has hatched,' he shouted louder.

'Yes, I heard, drive up and keep to the plan.'

'It must be a blinking goose.'

'Why are you still here?' Asked Helen.

Old Owl explained her mobility problem.

'So, once you speed up you can fly?'

'That's right,' Old Owl paced the lawn impatiently.

'I have an idea,' Helen dashed into the house. Some minutes later, with helmet, elbow and knee pads in place, she reappeared with her bike.

'Come on. I'm going to get you airborne.'

'But how? You can't fly.'

Helen lay on her tummy in front of the owl, 'just do as I say.'

'The Chosen One has gone mad, this is all going badly wrong'.

'Now turn around and walk backwards onto my head.'

'Totally loopy.' But she followed the instructions.

'Now, as I stand up, move forward on my head and try to remain upright.' With a struggle and steadying the helmet with her hands Helen wobbled to the perpendicular.

'You weigh a ton.'

'What's happening? What are you thinking?' Old Owl spread her wings to keep her balance.

'I'll explain as we go.' Helen pushed her bike through the garage to the front of the house.

'Just going for a bike ride, Dad,' she shouted.

'You be careful.'

'Now, I'm not sure this will work but it's worth a try. I'll cycle with you on my head and, as I speed up, spread your wings and, well, you know the rest.'

She was already on her bike pedalling and, as she accelerated, the weight transferred to Old Owl's fully expanded wings; she became lighter and lighter until she was in full independent flight.

It should be noted that a man fell from a ladder whilst watching this.

*

Bouncer and Mr Tolly approached the nest. 'Fly ahead and tell them to prepare for the landing'. Mr Tolly alerted Merlin and Judy.

'They're ready and waiting.'

'This is the tricky part', thought Bouncer. He slowed to a hover and this was more demanding than flying, his lungs were burning, his chest heaved. Suspended above the broad branch, he lowered the precious package slowly towards Merlin who was ready and waiting. He took the weight on his chest and enveloped the Royal Egg in his wings, then walked it gently through the opening.

Bouncer perched outside exhausted, his wings hung limply at his side.

'Well done, little bird, I don't think I would have managed without your help.' Mr Tolly lay as if dead.

'Bouncer come and see this,' Bouncer and Mr Tolly staggered into the nest. Judy had folded the shopping bag down at the top. Nestling in Merlin's embrace, a human baby slept peacefully.

'Not a goose, then,' said Mr Tolly.

'Old Owl has to be told. Mr Tolly, fly as quickly as you can and inform Old Owl, she'll know what to do.'

'What? My wings are falling off.'

'Just fly.'

He walked onto the beam and launched into the air, mumbling – 'nothing to do with me, this. And how did that stupid baby get into the egg anyway? There's stuff going on here that I just don't understand.'

He arrived, after a while, in the empty garden.

*

Old Owl usually had help landing at the nest, but was desperate to see if the Royal Egg had arrived safely. She aimed her descent straight at the narrow end of the broad branch, completed three somersaults and ended upside-down in the back of the nest.

When the dust had settled and she had established which was up and which was down, she focussed on an unfamiliar sound.

*

Mr Tolly searched everywhere but Old Owl was not to be found.

'I'd better return and tell them. They're bound to blame me and then definitely kill me.' "Lose Old Owl, eh? Off with his head." He made his way back to Greenwich Park.

*

'A human baby, well, well,' Old Owl stared at the little face.

'It has happened before, just the once, but the baby died. This little baby is going to survive ... it must.'

'Old Owl isn't there, I have searched the whole garden. She has gone ...'. Mr Tolly blinked into the nest.

'We need help. Birds can't raise human babies.'

'I could catch a mouse for it,' said Bouncer.

'A human baby wouldn't be able to digest a live mouse', said Judy, 'worms would be better, no bones, they wriggle straight down.'

'No, we need the Chosen One, Helen will know what to do. Who would be best to speak with her?' Old Owl glanced around the nest.

'Oh no,' Mr Tolly was listening outside, he lay on his back with his feet in the air. 'Why don't they just kill me?'

'Judy you go.'

'Thank heavens.' Mr Tolly relaxed.

'Take Mr Tolly with you, Helen seemed to like him. Go now.'

'Come on, Mr Tolly, it's not far as the crow flies.'

'Very funny,' he followed the crow through the trees and over the park wall.

Twins

They found Helen on the swing in her garden. Judy described the developments at the nest.

'Old Owl wondered if you have any ideas. Birds don't know how to care for human babies, you see, and we don't want it to die.'

Helen left the swing and paced back and forth, scratching her head. The birds were watching – she stopped abruptly and gave a little jump.

'No', she shook her head, turned and resumed the to-and-fro marching.

'Now listen, we have to find the baby a human mother. It needs milk, you see.' She rocked herself on the swing again. Her brain was in overdrive.

'Yes, of course, why didn't I think of that before?' She leapt from the swing, waking Mr Tolly and ran into the house.

'Mum, Dad, can we visit the twins?

'Strangely enough, Mark said we should drop by, Lucy is about to give birth and it's a home delivery' said Mum, 'she suggested we take the twins to the park for a while?'

'OK,' said Dad, 'give them a buzz and tell them we're on our way.' He folded his newspaper and Mum grabbed the phone.

'Ooooh quick' shouted Mum, 'Lucy is going into labour.'

'I'll just fetch my doll.'

'*Your doll*?', chimed Mum and Dad. Mum dropped the phone.

Helen retrieved her doll from the back of her bottom drawer. It was one of those rubbery lifelike ones.

'Hello stranger, I guessed you might come in handy one day.' She wrapped it in shawl and ran into the garden. She showed her two friends the doll.

'I have a plan, see you in the park.'

*

'Gerry across the road broke his arm, you know' said Dad as they drove.

'Oh dear, how did he manage that?', asked Mum.

'Fell off his ladder.'

'One should take safety precautions on ladders', advised Helen.

'He did, but he was distracted by a stunt rider on a bike with an eagle on her head.'

'Oh dear, poor man.'

Mark waited at the door with the twins ready for their walk.

'She has started. The midwife's here.' He left the children on the doorstep and closed the door.

Martin and Jess were four years old and excited about the forthcoming event, but just as pleased to be going to the park with Helen.

It was a short walk to the park and Helen held the doll carefully, rehearsing for the real thing a little later – providing everything went to plan.

Once in the park, she searched for Judy and Mr Tolly.

She caught a glimpse of them by the duck pond. 'I wonder where the oak tree with the nest is', she thought.

Judy began hopping towards a thicket while Mr Tolly ate some bread. She disappeared into the cover of the bushes, Helen followed. Her absence went unnoticed as the others fed the ducks.

'Where's the nest?'

'This way.' Helen followed the crow and they halted at the base of the oak tree.

'This is the tree, I've never seen it from this angle before', said Judy, looking up.

'Judy, I know where I'm going to take the baby.' She outlined her strategy, explaining that it wasn't watertight and some fine-tuning might be necessary.

'I don't know how I'll explain where the baby came from, but I'll have to play that by ear. Can you ask Bouncer to lower the baby to me in the shopping bag?

'That might be tricky. What if he's seen by humans? An owl carrying a human baby in a shopping bag ...'

'Mm, that's a point. Perhaps you could ask Merlin to create a diversion by the pond.'

'I'll see what I can do.' Judy flew up to the nest.

*

'Push ... push', encouraged the midwife.

*

Merlin launched towards the duck pond whilst Bouncer, assisted by Old Owl, dragged the shopping bag containing its precious cargo out onto the branch. Mr Tolly, sufficiently nourished, joined them.

'What's Merlin doing? I think he's flipped his lid.'

Merlin was dive-bombing the humans around the duck pond. Dad was attempting to photograph him with his mobile phone.

Bouncer began the lift, not far this time, and straight down.

'Be careful, you're right on the edge' warned Mum. Merlin dived straight for him. Dad leaned back, peering into the screen, a touch more ... splash.

Down and down came the baby in the bag. Helen met the package with outstretched arms. She removed it from the bag and wrapped it in the shawl.

'You're a lovely baby, now please, please don't cry,' she took a moment to gaze at this most unusual baby.

Having hidden the doll and the bag in the undergrowth, she emerged unobserved by the drama at the pond.

*

The midwife gave the baby to Mark.

'There you are, my dear, a lovely baby boy. I'll make some tea.'

*

'Dad? What happened?' Dad stood dripping, cold from the smelly pond water.

'Helen, take him to Mark's house, he'll be arrested walking about like that on his own. I'll stay here with the twins.'

'OK Mum, be back soon. Come on Dad. What happened?'

'I was trying to take a picture of that rabid vulture; it was attacking everything in sight.'

'Good old Merlin,' thought Helen.

Mark came to the door carrying the new-born baby.

'A boy,' he announced in a whisper, 'What happened to you, Andy? You're drenched. Lucy is sleeping, don't make a noise.' He put his finger to his lips.

'You need a shower, come up stairs and I'll find you some dry clothes.' Dad followed Mark up the stairs.

'Helen slipped silently into the nursery where Lucy lay sleeping soundly.

The final episode of Helen's plan to provide the product of the Royal Egg with the nurture to support its survival was nearing completion. Everything had unfolded as Old Owl had anticipated, the messenger and the Chosen One had played their part as if born to the role.

Helen removed the shawl from the baby, gently lifted the quilt and laid the baby close to its new mother, a dried leaf fell to the carpet.

She closed the door silently behind her and with the shawl around her neck like a scarf, shouted softly through the shower room door.

'Dad, I'm going back to the park to find the others and tell them about the new baby.'

'OK' said Dad.

'See you later, Mark,' and she was gone.

Helen retrieved her doll from the shrubbery beneath the oak and joined Mum and the little ones.

'It's a boy,' she smiled at Martin and Jess, 'you have a baby brother' she said. 'Here, you can have this.' She handed the doll to Jess.

'No thanks, I have a real baby waiting for me at home.'

'Two, actually,' breathed Helen. She tucked the shawl under her arm and, when no one was looking, dumped the doll head first into a bin. They walked back to the house.

*

Helen's dad, dry and rigged out in some of Marks clothes, crept down the stairs.

'Wait here with the baby and I'll see if Lucy is awake, the little chap looks hungry.' Mark handed the baby to Andy.

Lucy sat up in bed, baby at breast.

'Mark you shouldn't have left the baby in bed with me while I slept. I might have rolled on to him.'

'Andy, come in – and ask the midwife to come too.'

Andy entered the nursery holding the new-born baby.

'What's that you're holding?' said Lucy.

'Who's that you're feeding?' said Andy.

*

That evening, in one corner of the nest stood Old Owl, opposite sat Helen's doll, one eye open and the other closed. Bouncer had flown it to the nest after the gates to the park were locked and dusk fell.

'There's work to be done and it is *owl work*, Judy and Mr Tolly, you are day birds, return to your nests and roost.' Old Owl sent them their separate ways.

She continued, 'before we leave for the ceremony I suggest that Mr Tolly be spared the traditional fate of the messenger. I also propose that he be elevated to the rank of Honorary Owl.'

'I agree', said Bouncer 'he was a great help flying the Royal Egg, he bore his fair share of the weight.'

'So that means he'll now be known as 'Mr Tolly HO', smiled Merlin.

*

Helen, her mum and the twins tiptoed into the now crowded nursery. The midwife seemed more confused than the parents.

Lucy smiled to see the new arrivals from the park.

'It's twins' she said.

'I told her to have a scan,' said Mark.

'It'll be alright Mark, we're experts at rearing twins and this time we have Jess and Martin to give a hand. And if you look closely, you'll see that they're identical twins.'

'It's a miracle', said Helen's mum.

'You're not wrong there.' Mumbled Helen softly to herself. She stooped and picked up a stray leaf from the carpet.

***

It was midnight, the park was closed. Grouped in the moonlight around the oaks were hundreds of owls of all shapes and sizes. They encircled a dozen or so ten-year-old owls perched on the original prostrate Queen Elizabeth I Oak for the solemn occasion.

The Annual Marking and Remembering Ceremony.

Old Owl addressed the flock of blinking eyes. 'In a hundred years there'll be a new Royal Egg, a new century begins and a new oak stands ready. We make a mark with our beak in the trunk.'

She stood on a small branch of the little oak tree.

'This has to be done every year at the time of the falling leaves'. She shaped a deep cut through the bark with her beak, stepping back to view the fresh wound on the modest trunk.

'In ten years there'll be ten such scars and, each year, the cut has to be refreshed because the tree will try to heal itself. Your duty as owls is to continue this work, led by Merlin and Bouncer, and ensure that the message is passed to the next generation of owls. In ten years, one long scar across these ten has to be worked.'

Our duty is to count the next hundred years and pass on the word. We'll watch over the baby – the fruit of the Royal Egg – but we have no further involvement. Now go about your nightly business. We meet again next year.

*

Mr Tolly awoke the next morning in the familiar surroundings of the bridge. Trains rattled above and chattering children walked under the bridge to school.

'What have you been up to these past few days? asked Mrs Tolly.

'Oh, nothing much. I can't remember.'

'Helen – breakfast is on the table', shouted Mum.

She sat up in bed and looked out of the window onto the garden. The plant had withered to nothing.

'Mum, I had a really weird dream last night.'

'Oh, what was it about?

'I can't remember.'

Judy preened her glossy wings and, with perfect recall calculated her response to yesterday's activities. She remembered every tiny detail.

*

Mark sat with little Martin and Jess on his lap; they looked proudly at Lucy holding the new twins.

Behind them on the sideboard, the tropical fish pushed against the glass, their tails wagging. An array of birds from the park perched on a branch outside and looked through the window.

Ed's Rat Tales

King Silver

'Calm down, pull yourselves together,' said Bouncer. 'Old Owl won't see you until there's some proper order.'

King Silver and his committee of squirrels found it difficult to be calm since hearing the news of their forthcoming demise. The clamour at Owl headquarters attracted more and more curious onlookers and the broad beam filled up to overflowing.

Silver, his tail twitching uncontrollably, turned and standing tall with his paws downturned, signalled silence to his committee and the birds beyond.

'That's better, now wait.' Bouncer turned slowly and walked into the nest.

*

Ed the rat became aware of the commotion as he prepared for one of his story-telling forums. He was about to tell the tale of Mr Noon's cat and the Gold Award racing pigeon that it ate. (He enjoyed mentioning that the Gold Award was for racing and not gourmet excellence). The mid-May sun shone promisingly on the nest box where he lived and Ed wriggled his bottom on its roof, which doubled as a stage, cleared his throat and eyed his gathering audience but the rumpus at Old Owl's headquarters prevented him from even starting.

His normally attentive listeners, mainly birds but squirrels too, deserted him, only Alf and Crispin remained and as neither of them wanted to miss out on any Greenwich Park gossip, Ed asked the brothers for a lift.

Ed was the only flying rat in the park. He moistened his prominent incisors with his tongue then lay flat on his tummy with his front legs stretched forward and Crispin stood so that Ed could grab his legs firmly. Alf grabbed the tip of the truncated rat tail and off they flew. This was Ed's preferred method of transport ... he had trained his two pigeon friends and they practiced until they could travel the length and breadth of the park and beyond with ease. So, with Crispin leading the way and Alf bringing up the rear, they made their way to the branch high in the nearby oak tree. Unable to find a space on the crowded beam, Crispin and Alf gently alighted on a smaller branch above, and the three settled to watch the goings on.

*

'What does King Silver want?' whispered Old Owl, 'it must be important for him to turn to us for help. I'd better come and see.' She glanced at the child's doll wedged snugly against the back of the nest.

'You wait here,' she said. Despite its unhearing ears and glass eyes, one staring ahead and the other fixed shut, Old Owl had developed the habit of talking to the doll, of telling it her innermost secrets. Bouncer stepped aside and Old Owl toddled into the May sunlight. Her eyes blinked at the sharp rays and she scanned the crowd that clapped and tweeted and cooed.

King Silver bowed, 'Old Owl, it's been a long time, we must speak, I need to tap into your superior wisdom,' he glanced at the gathered birds, 'in private'.

'Merlin, Bouncer, you know what to do.' The owl brothers took to the air and began chasing the birds away. Instinctively, Crispin and Alf joined the exodus leaving poor Ed isolated on the branch above. Desperately looking for an escape, he only had seconds, for if the owl brothers returned to discover a rat spying on them he would end up as owl fodder. He ran to the end of the branch and looked down – it was too far to jump. He thought it rotten luck that he lacked the agility of the fleeing squirrels. He turned, racing like a greyhound, and, just as he approached the main trunk of the mighty oak, he noticed a small hole where the branch met the upright. Within a flash he had dived head first into the opening. He landed on a soft bed of wood dust, he could not believe his luck. Ed stood up and looked around. Light shone in from the small opening.

‘I’ll be safe here until dark,’ he thought. A smile exposed two rat teeth, yellowed with age.

‘I’m such a clever rat,’ a little song formed in his head and he began to explore his hideaway.

‘Cleverer than a cat, smarter than an owl, safe until it’s dark ...’ he hummed softly to himself as he sniffed around the hole. His sniffing suddenly stopped and he ran through the words of his ditty ‘safe until it’s dark ... owls ... dark ... night’ his smile returned and he continued exploring, ‘safe until morning, when all the owls are snoring.’

He searched for a place to sleep and found an especially soft spot just to one side. He wriggled on his back to form a rat-shaped bed and went to sleep.

Now, a common dream is that of falling and Ed was experiencing such a dream right now ... only it was not a dream. The bed of wood dust fell away, and down plummeted Ed through the inside of the trunk. He tumbled only a short distance and landed most awkwardly straddling a hard seam of oak that had not yet rotted. He sat, as if on a bicycle, but a bicycle with no saddle.

Even hearty oaks are vulnerable to wear and tear and during its four hundred years, pockets of rot had mined secret tunnels in its massive body. Ed’s hiding place was similar to the large nest that Old Owl had moved into many years earlier. It had formed in the same way, too, by rain collecting in the little hollow where the branch met the trunk and gradually eating away at the hard wood.

***

‘Come inside,’ said Old Owl. King Silver and his entourage followed her into the nest. Now it was the turn of the squirrel’s eyes to adapt to the light change and, as they did, they focussed on the pink face of the doll at the back of the nest.

‘Where’ve they gone?’ said Old Owl, ‘I thought they wanted to talk. Strange creatures, I never did understand squirrels. First they want a meeting ... then they’re gone.’

Silver was the first to return, peeping into the dark and waiting for reassurance that the apparition lurking at the back of the nest was not harmful to squirrels. Two more joined him but the others were not seen for days.

Ed could hear every word of the conversation. The shaft, down which he had fallen, passed behind the owl headquarters and the sharp wedge of oak protruded from the back wall of the nest. Leaning against the wall on the other side sat Helen's doll, mere inches from Ed's nose.

He held his breath. He could not move, his legs were jammed and his position made him very uncomfortable. If he could hear Old Owl so clearly, then any noise he made would be detected. He resigned himself to the fact that not only was he uncomfortable but he had to be quiet about it. Calling for help was certainly out of the question unless he wanted to end up in an owl's stomach ... which he did not.

'What is that?' asked Silver, 'it looks like a human baby.'

'It's Helen's doll, a gift from the Chosen One, you wouldn't understand and I haven't time to explain now, so King Silver ... how can I help you?'

'Poison,' said Silver.

Ed licked his lips.

'The park keepers have been instructed to poison the squirrel population of Greenwich Park.'

'Well, don't eat it,' said Bouncer who was listening at the door. 'If you know about it, then just don't eat it.'

Ed suppressed a chuckle.

'It's not that simple,' replied Silver, unable to take his eyes from the doll which still unnerved him. 'The adult squirrels will obey such an order, but the young ... well, you know what they're like, tell them not to do something and they go and do it.'

'Well, tell them to eat it ... then they won't.'

'That's enough Bouncer, you're not helping.'

Ed stifled a guffaw.

'Why poison the squirrels?' asked Old Owl.

'I've no idea. We're very popular with the visitors. People come from all over the world to see us. I can't understand it.'

Ed was only half listening, the mention of poison had made him hungry and he was far from food of any kind. If only he could get a message to Alf and Crispin, they could haul him up on a piece of string from his collection of old conker strings. Now, rats are clever and Ed was cleverer than most, having developed the skill of thinking his way through tricky situations, but he had to admit that to escape from this was going to take some pretty powerful thinking.

Old Owl's sharp hearing would detect any movement and, these days, she hardly ever left the proximity of the nest and was never alone. A feeling of despair began to overwhelm him and he resigned himself to the prospect of death by starvation – starvation or discomfort. But inspiration was nigh when King Silver said 'tell me about Helen's doll.'

Old Owl had always found squirrels irritating, but the thought of Greenwich Park without them concerned her. More than that, if the poison worked its way into the food chain via mice and voles, for example it would eventually find its way to owls. Poison and humans were an unstable combination.

Ed knew of 'Helen and the Royal Egg' but had never heard the full story. A telling by Old Owl would be worth hearing, so, having no choice anyway, he put his despair to one side and listened to the story.

By the time she had finished, Ed had the key to his escape ... a very daring and highly risky escape. He had known of Mr Tolly's involvement that day, but not of the high regard shown towards Crispin and Alf's rotund father "Mr Tolly HO".

He knew precisely how he would outwit Old Owl, the wisest creature in Greenwich Park.

Edwina

During the hush that followed the story, Ed seized the chance to put the first part of his plan into action. In a loud echoing voice he said ...

'Mr Tolly ... send for him ... he, and only he, can save the squirrels of Greenwich Park.'

King Silver and his followers could not flee, the opening was blocked by Bouncer, but panic they could and panic they did. They sprinted around the cavernous nest ... up the walls ... across the ceiling in the darkened space until, calmed by the stunned silence of the owls, they settled ... and all eyes focused on Helen's doll.

Old Owl, who was normally at ease with words, pointed with her wing to the opening, her beak opened and closed but no words emerged, until...

'Mr Tolly ... fetch Mr Tolly ... send Judy ... check the bridge at Greenwich Station ... scour the park ... he must be found. Helen's doll has at last spoken and she must be obeyed.'

Ed laughed silently into his paw.

A search soon found Mr Tolly napping on the far side of the duck pond. He had had a fill of bread and was sleeping it off.

'What have I done? I haven't done anything. It wasn't me. It was very likely Elvis. A pigeon is innocent until proven guilty.'

'Be quiet', said Judy as they flew the short distance to the oak.

'Old Owl only wants to speak with you. Although I don't see why.'

As they entered the nest, Mr Tolly bowed into the darkness at anyone or anything that he thought needed bowing to.

'How nice, how do you do, Old Owl? What mild weather we're having, almost summery, wouldn't you say?' He nodded to the squirrels and, as his eyes adjusted to the dark, greeted King Silver with an extra low bow.

'I need to be alone with Mr Tolly,' said Helen's doll.

'Who was that? It sounded like Ed ...'

'Edwina, correct, Mr Tolly, my name is Edwina. Witness his depth of knowledge, oh, lowly creatures, now leave us to debate the matter of the poison.'

The squirrels backed out and Old Owl ushered Judy and the owl brothers onto the branch. King Silver and company were dismissed and told that the case was being dealt and that they would be informed of the outcome.

'Mr Tolly, please ensure that we can't be overheard, it's a grave matter that threatens the squirrel population of Greenwich Park and secrecy is paramount.'

Mr Tolly walked to the opening and shooed the potential eavesdroppers to the end of the broad branch.

'You heard him ... her ... Edwina in there ... paramount, shoo.' He turned and marched importantly back into the darkness. 'Ed, what are you doing inside that doll,' whispered Mr Tolly, 'if Old Owl discovers ...'

'I know. Don't you think I don't know that? I'm not inside the doll I'm behind it.' Mr Tolly peered cautiously behind the doll, but there was no rat and no space big enough for a rat.

'Where? I can't see you in this light.'

'I'm behind the oak panelling, I fell down from above. You need to fetch Alf and Crispin to rescue me.'

'Alf and Crispin? What can they do?'

'Come closer and I'll explain.'

So, in whispers, Ed explained about his fall, about being stuck and about the plot to poison the squirrels. He then went on to describe his escape plan with Alf and Crispin hauling him to safety at the end of a conker string. 'Once my legs are free, they can pull me the rest of the way, the wood is rotten behind here and there's no place to grip.'

'But Old Owl's bound to smell a rat ... no offence, nothing to do with your personnel hygiene, but while we're on the subject ...'

'What are you babbling on about? Look, make an excuse and say you need to involve your two sons. Fetch Alf and Crispin and I'll outline the finer details of the escape to them ... and bring Elvis ... and on your way out, send in Old Owl, alone, now go.'

He wriggled his toes in order to allow the blood to flow and tested for leg movement before Old Owl returned.

'Edwina, you sent for me.' The power shift could be detected in Old Owl's voice, enhancing Ed's confidence. Remembering to engage his dolly voice, he said *'Old Owl, Mr Tolly's rounding up my team of advisers, which consists of some pigeons, a rat and a sparrow hawk.'* Ed knew that Elvis would have Mercedes close by.

'A rat? A sparrow hawk?' Old Owl was surprised but she was more interested in the phenomenon of the speaking and, more critically, listening doll.

'Ahem,' she cleared her throat as if weighing her words carefully, 'you do realise the significance of the subject matter that I've revealed to you over these past months, don't you, Edwina?' Ed replied with a neutral *"mmm"* which he hoped would cover all scenarios. Old Owl continued, 'because until I discuss it thoroughly with Merlin, I wish the knowledge of my forthcoming death to stay between the two of us. Do you understand?'

'Of course, Old Owl, mum's the word.'

'What was she talking about? Death? If she was dying, how did she know? And what exactly has she told me? Should I say that I've only just become a conscious being? That I've heard nothing?' All of these questions raced around his head, just as the squirrels had raced around the owls nest earlier. He inhaled, deciding that he would plead ignorance.

'Midsummer would be nice,' she said as if planning a holiday, 'the summer solstice might be my last day and Merlin will become the new "Old Owl". You knew it would be Merlin, didn't you?' She spoke warmly as if the doll was an intimate confidant of many years.'

'Well yes, I did guess ...'

'Bouncer is wonderful, strong and dependable but he has the wrong sort of brain to lead. He'll support his brother, of that I'm sure. Edwina, can I ask you something?'

'Certainly' Ed's discomfort was taking on new dimensions.

'When I'm ... gone ... will you still be here, listening to Merlin as you've listened to me? Oh, I know you can't do anything, but if I knew that you were still here; well, it would make my passing so much easier.' She turned her back to the doll and looked towards the light.

'It means so much having someone to talk to.' Before Ed could conjure up another noncommittal reply, and to his great relief, the rescue party alighted on the beam outside. Old Owl met them at the entrance and, noticing the absence of a rat, waved them in and joined the others at the far end of the branch.

'Ed, you still there?' whispered Mr Tolly.

'No, I've turned into a woodpecker and pecked my way out.'

'Tut, tut, sarcasm is the lowest form of wit, you know.'

'Of course I'm still here. Who's with you?'

'Crispin, Alf and Elvis, Mercedes is but a coo away.'

'Good, come close so that you can all hear.'

Passing

An essential part of Ed's plan was for the owls nest to be deserted whilst the rescue took place. Elvis would lead a reconnaissance team consisting of Bouncer, Merlin, Judy, Mr Tolly and, critically, – Old Owl to the gardener's workshop area in search of the poison. Alf and Crispin had to fetch the longest conker string they could find, or tie two together, so that it would be long enough to reach him from the hole above. The next part of the plan illustrates the devious workings of Ed's brain. He wanted the string to be a permanent fixture so that he could return to spy on the controlling forces of Greenwich Park. Ed did not mention this detail to his rescue party, but he reckoned that, as the voice and ears of Edwina the doll, he could influence that power. The string would be fixed at the top with a short piece of strong bamboo jammed into the hole so that it was invisible from the outside.

He spoke softly into the wood.

'Elvis, the biggest hurdle will be persuading Old Owl to go with you. Tell her that these are instructions from Edwina; send her to me if she refuses. Any questions?'

Elvis gathered his crew outside and debriefed them. Ed was right about Old Owl's reluctance to fly, but Helen's doll had become such an inspiration that she went without too much fuss. Bouncer assisted her until she flew unaided.

***

Elvis and Mr Tolly perched on the solid wooden gates of the fenced area as the reconnaissance party circled above. 'What's wrong with Old Owl?' asked Mr Tolly, 'look at her wing movements, something's wrong.'

Judy swooped down and joined them. 'Old Owl's tiring, she must rest, it was a mistake to bring her.'

'Let her rest, then, perhaps she's hungry,' said Mr Tolly.

'It's not that simple, she can't take off from the ground, she has to launch from a high position, the roof of that shed would be perfect.'

Old Owl began losing height, Bouncer flew to the rescue trying position his strong body under her heavy frame, but he was too late. There was no time to coordinate the wing beat and they crashed together in a heap and rolled under a parked tractor. Bouncer gently dusted the gravel from Old Owl's back with his wings, but she lay still.

The door of the canteen opened and gardeners in their green dungarees spilled into the yard. Some pushed wheel barrows, others carried hoes and rakes as they set off into the park to resume their spring projects. The tractor driver hauled himself into the cab, the engine turned with a whine and then sprang into life. The noise ripped into Merlin's ears ... but Old Owl heard nothing. The gears engaged with a crunch and the tractor left the yard.

*

Ed the rat waited patiently for the return of Crispin and Alf and before long he could hear noises above and the changing shadows told him of their arrival.

He looked up in time to see the conker accelerating towards him, but not in time to avoid it. The words *'you should've removed the conker from the string'* formed in his head, but never made it to his voice box. His eyes closed just in time for the space between them to bounce the conker half way up again. He reflected later that had he not been so firmly stuck, he would have been propelled to the bottom of the tree. Fortunately, not all of his wits had been knocked into his feet and he managed to catch the conker on the rebound.

'OK, haul me up' he said, his head spinning.

Neither pigeon beaks nor pigeon physiques are designed with tug-of-war in mind. Had the brothers pulled evenly and in step, Ed's ascent would have been smooth, but when Alf let go in order to renew his grip, Crispin, under the weight, tottered back towards the hole and Ed started down again. Alf reacted quickly and grabbed the string, but Crispin began telling him off … which of course you can't do with a beak full of conker string … and so Ed's descent began once more.

The yo-yo rodent went up and down, and whilst he did, he speculated on the relative tranquillity of an owl's stomach.

Eventually he made it to the top and emerged into the sunlight.

*

Bouncer lay across Old Owl, his wings spread to conceal her from predators. Owls are night birds and shy, and, with the tractor gone, they were exposed. The foreman crossed the empty yard, slowing as he saw the two owls huddled together. He approached the tangled mass of feathers inquisitively and, as he did, the dive-bombing began, first Elvis, followed closely by Mercedes, Merlin and Judy. Shocked and frightened, the man retreated to the safety of the workshop. Throughout the attack, Bouncer lay motionless, covering Old Owl protectively.

Merlin joined him. 'Let me see.'

Bouncer slowly withdrew his wings and folded them to his side, he knew she was dead and when Merlin saw Old Owl lying in the gravel, he knew it, too.

Birds and animals accept death as a natural part of life, however, this was Old Owl and Merlin and Bouncer stood gazing at their dead leader.

'Get away! Shoo!' The foreman charged, an umbrella held aloft and a broom under his arm like a gallant knight of old.

Instinctively Merlin and Bouncer beat their powerful wings and sprang into flight. They left the enclosure and flew towards the Owl headquarters.

Everyone but Mr Tolly followed, he watched the foreman approach the dead owl and watched him discard the umbrella and broom. He then_watched him lower himself to his knees and place his hands gently on the dead owl.

He heard the whisper 'you poor thing, what have they done to you?' Mr Tolly watched the man spread Old Owl's wing carefully and murmur words of wonder. He saw him close the wings and smooth the feathers into place. And Mr Tolly saw the sparkle of dew trickle from the man's eye and fall to the ground.

Stuffed

News of Old Owls death spread like pollen on the wind and the busy chatter was of nothing else. Within the park walls and beyond, as far as Oxleas Woods to the south. East and west along the banks of the River Thames and even the other side of the river, north of the Cutty Sark, speculation of Old Owl's successor spread from mouth to mouth and from beak to beak.

Who would be the next "Old Owl"?

The deciding factor emerged from a most surprising source ...

One of the baby twins, at only seven months old, had spoken a single word ... "Merlin" ... he pronounced the word as clear as any adult ... "Merlin".

Mark cooed into the cot 'dad, dad, dad.' But the baby repeated his word over and over 'Merlin' and then the budgie copied him, 'Merlin', the birds in the trees outside heard it and repeated 'Merlin' and they flew to the park spreading the word 'Merlin ... Merlin' spreading it throughout the park and beyond. The chant was 'Merlin ... Merlin'.

There were, of course, many other owl families who could have challenged for the role of leader, but as the chant spread, their ambitions shrank and there were no pretenders to the crownless post.

*

The Owl Headquarters had been besieged by curious creatures of all sorts. But away from the hustle and bustle of Old Owls nest ... another meeting was in progress. The feeling in Ed's legs and feet had returned and his tummy was full. He sat on the roof of his nest box as Elvis retold the drama of Old Owl's death with Mr Tolly listening thoughtfully.

Elvis concluded '... and as Bouncer and Merlin stood over Old Owl, the man returned, this time he was armed and tried to kill them.'

Mr Tolly tried to interject, 'I don't think he ...'

'He charged with a sweeping tool, you know the type, a stick with a dead hedgehog on the end ...'

'It wasn't really like that ...'

'He needs to be dealt with,' continued Elvis, ignoring Mr Tolly's objections, 'but that will have to wait. Old Owl's death has moved attention away from the poison and we must resume the search. I'm beginning to suspect that this same man is behind the planned massacre.'

Mr Tolly's protestation 'He didn't seem like that sort of man,' went unheeded.

'We need to talk with Merlin and Bouncer, but have you seen it over there? How can we possibly get a message to them?'

'Through Edwina of course' said Ed, 'the string is in place, everything is ready, I just need Crispin and Alf to fly me there.'

'Your approach branch is covered with birds of all sorts and they're not to be frightened off by Mercedes. We'll have to find the poison without Merlin and Bouncer. Mr Tolly, fetch Alf and Crispin.'

Murmuring something about 'he seemed such a nice man' Mr Tolly went to find his sons, the rat transporters.

*

The roof to the workshop proved a suitable landing platform. Alf and Crispin rotated their wings to break speed and as they slowed, Ed's skinny back legs began paddling the air until they touched the black felt roof. Alf let the rat tail drop and Ed released his grip on Crispin's legs for a safe landing.

There were several buildings, some small sheds and the large brick-built office and canteen where the workers ate their lunch. 'I can smell it already,' said Ed with a nostalgic smile.

'Shush' said Mr Tolly as the door to the main building opened and the green-clad men and women poured into the yard. It was going-home time for the gardeners. Hidden from view they listened as the humans walked within earshot.

'The birds were acting strangely today ...'

'Not just the birds ...'

'First they kill that poor owl ...'

'And the chanting ...'

'I've never heard anything like it ...'

'We might be in for a storm ...'

The foreman was the last to leave and he carried a black plastic bin liner containing something heavy. He padlocked the gate and walked from the park to his car.

'Carry on without me' said Mr Tolly. He followed the foreman.

'OK Ed, give us a demonstration of how sensitive your nose is, find the poison' said Elvis. Ed thrust his twitching nose aloft. Alf and Crispin giggled; Ed's outstretched neck pulled the fur tight tugging his lower lip to expose a full set of ivories. He circled on his hind legs with his nose in the air and his eyes began to bulge as they did before his rehabilitation.

'Warm ...' he said 'cold, cold ...' then he ran the other way like a wind-up toy on wheels, 'warm, warm.' The giggling stopped when Ed plunged over the edge of the roof, then started again as the young pigeons saw that he was not injured, it seemed he had been upgraded to a radio-controlled toy programmed to home in on a signal. The wheels stopped outside one of the smaller sheds and the small rodent pointed with his nose and the claw of his index finger.

'It's in there,' he said. Anyone who had witnessed the performance would not argue.

The structure was nothing more than a large garden shed. An examination revealed that it was in good condition with no rotten wood or gaps for Ed to squeeze through. The door was padlocked top and bottom and there were no windows.

*

Mr Tolly followed the foreman's car through the streets of Greenwich. He perched high on a mast of the Cutty Sark, waiting for the car as it moved slowly through the traffic. From the ancient tea clipper in its dry dock, he saw the Thames and watched the tourists go about their business.

The car eventually stopped at a taxidermist shop. He watched the foreman retrieve the bin liner from the boot and enter the shop. From the roof of the car he saw the sack being emptied and, as he suspected, it was Old Owl's remains that lay on the counter. Mr Tolly knew of the doctors who healed broken birds and animals and he knew of butchers who sold them for humans to eat. This shop did not seem to fit either category. From the roof of the car, he could see the stuffed animals, perfect, but motionless. 'How did they remain still for so long?' He attempted one of the poses, copying a peregrine falcon, its wings poised mid-flight, its eyes scanning the floor of the shop as if a mouse might be up for grabs. He toppled forward, 'they must practice for hours,' he thought. The door of the shop opened with a 'ching' and the foreman walked towards the car. A lingering glance connected bird and man.

*

'I can gnaw my way in', said Ed, 'see these teeth?' Crispin and Alf giggled again as Ed drew back his lips, 'cut anything with these teeth, watch.' Within a minute and a half, he had made a small hole. 'Give me ten minutes and I'll be in there.'

'And?' said Elvis.

'Fly me up to the roof again and I'll explain my plan. I don't like it down here.' Ed had noticed a disconcerting smell of fox.

Ed lay on his side with his head resting on one paw, Elvis and the two young pigeons listened.

'If they propose poisoning squirrels, then I say we should poison them.' Ed looked to Elvis for a response and as there was none he continued.

'How do we do that? You may well ask. Living as I have, in a house, you get to know a thing or two about humans. They don't drink from the duck pond you may have noticed, nor do they pull worms from the ground, nor bury acorns for the winter, no, they're far too organized for that. Humans store food in their houses, in boxes and tins and cold places. We just need to take a little poison and mix it with their food ... in there.' He pointed to the canteen. 'That's where they eat. I can smell it,' his nose twitched.

'So we kill the gardeners, how will that help? More gardeners will come with more poison and we're back where we started,' said Elvis.

'A small amount of poison won't kill a human, it'll only make him ill. As soon as that happens they won't work with the poison.'

'This is a radical step; we need to check it out with Merlin and Bouncer before going ahead,' said Elvis.

*

The next day a council of war met to work out a strategy. All the big guns were present, Merlin, Bouncer and Judy represented the new regime, Ed had clambered down the conker string and waited patiently behind the doll and Mr Tolly and Elvis would tell of Ed the rat's detective work and the discovery of the poison. Elvis would also attempt to establish Ed as a *bona fide* member of the project team so that he would be comfortable in the presence of owls and not feel like an item on the menu.

*

The baby from the Royal Egg and his family made their way to the park for a picnic.

Samuel was his real name, but everyone called him Blue, even strangers who met Mark and Lucy walking the twins in the pram commented on their eyes, Samuel's large, hauntingly blue eyes and Joseph's strikingly beautiful blue-green eyes. The colour of their eyes was the only difference in the otherwise identical twins. Martin and Rosamond laughed and giggled at the slow progress the family made as they walked to the park.

*

Elvis had told Merlin and co. of the stash of poison in the shed and of Ed's ability to break in, outlining the idea to steal a small amount in order to contaminate the gardener's food.

'Good work,' said Merlin 'but poisoning the gardener's food? What do you think, Judy?'

'It's wrong and it won't solve the problem ...'

'Why?' asked Edwina the doll.

Judy turned suspiciously towards the doll.

'Ah, still with us, eh? I thought Old Owl might have taken your spirit with her to the next world. Well, oh wise plastic one ... it won't solve the problem because we don't know what the problem is. Until we know *why* the humans want to kill the squirrels, we won't be able to find an answer. So, Edwina, why do the humans want to eliminate the squirrels? Can you answer that? Define the problem accurately and a solution will follow.'

Ed hadn't expected such a robust opposition to his plan. But he could think on his feet and retorted, *'Send Ed the rat on this simple errand and he'll surely find the answer. Ed the wonder rat sniffed out the poison and I warrant that he, together with Mr Tolly and his pigeon friends, will penetrate the evil mind of the leader of the green-clad gardeners.'* He finished with an indignant flourish that almost sent him plunging beyond the reach of the conker string.

'Oh,' said Judy turning to Merlin, 'it seems strange to me that the answer to all of our problems is a rat whom we've never met. Where is this wonder rat? Produce him.'

Merlin, surprised at Judy's animosity towards the doll, said.

'What do you say, Mr Tolly? Can you and Ed the rat establish the motive behind the poisoning? Because Judy is right, I think that if we poisoned the gardeners and their leader ... they would simply change tactics and set traps or come with their guns to shoot the squirrels. What would we do then? We have no guns.'

Mr Tolly had it in his mind to defend the foreman but what evidence did he have? A moment's eye contact, that's all, and what about Old Owl in the bin liner? So, he drew himself tall and pointed with his wing to the light.

'We'll find the reason for the squirrel hatred and report back as soon as we have a result. Ed the rat's absence can easily be explained. He has a keen sense of self-preservation and avoids hunting birds and animals. Ed is critical to the success of the mission, and I request freedom of passage for him.'

'If by "freedom of passage" you mean we won't eat him, I'll allow such a guarantee, providing your little team can establish the motives behind the threat to the squirrels,' said Merlin.

*

In the flower gardens, at a spot warmed by the gentle May sun, the family settled to enjoy a picnic. Mark played shuttlecocks with the older twins and Lucy absent-mindedly flicked bread crumbs to the birds, an opportunity for Mr Tolly to take in a quick snack. So whilst his sons flew Ed to the yard and Elvis updated Mercedes, he alighted gently and began competing for the crumbs. Immediately on landing, he felt the vibrations, the same ones transmitted from the Royal Egg in the garden. He left the scrambling melee of pigeons to perch on the pram handle and at once became mesmerized by a pair of blue eyes. *'Speak to the foreman, he will understand you.'*

'You're the baby aren't you ... the baby from the Royal Egg.'

'I am, my work has started. Listen carefully, there's little time, my mum won't like a pigeon so close to her young. There are too many grey squirrels, that's why there are plans to kill them, not all of them just some. But there's a better way, a natural way. The foreman will know what to do, he's thinking along those lines already but needs encouragement, he argued against poisoning but was outvoted.'

Lucy turned at the sound of Blue's gurgling and shooed the pigeon away.

Mr Tolly made the short dash to the yard and searched frantically for his partners. He found them high in a tree spying on the gardeners in the busy yard.

'I know the reason,' he said, 'I've spoken to the baby from the Royal Egg ... I need to find the foreman.' And off he flew.

'Your father worries me sometimes' said Ed. 'Where's he going? What's he doing?'

They watched as Mr Tolly swooped towards the main building and perched outside a window peering through the glass, moving from window to window. He checked the whole length of the building until, at last, he saw the foreman inside alone at his desk.

Mr Tolly flew in through the open window and landed on the filing cabinet and, without hesitating, he introduced himself.

'How do you do, my name is Mr Tolly, I'm told you'll be able to understand me,' he said with a low bow. It wasn't until he pulled himself upright that he noticed the animals and birds. Motionless figures like the ones in the shop, a jay, a weasel, a fox, dozens of stuffed creatures displayed in every corner and on every surface of the office.

The foreman at first looked uncomfortable and then began laughing. He went first to the window

'OK, very funny ...' and then to the door 'most amusing, highly entertaining ...' but no one was there.

'What's going on?' He closed the door and sat down staring at the pigeon. He gave a nervous giggle and decided to play along with what he believed to be a practical joke.

'So, you're Mr Tolly and yes, of course I can understand every word you say.'

'Good, I rather wondered for a moment, it's about the squirrels and the poison. Blue said you knew another way, a better way.'

The man watched every word and every syllable that emanated from the bird's beak.

'You're real,' he said 'fly around the office and land on the desk.' Mr Tolly did as requested, 'stand on one leg ... perch on my hand.'

'I'm not a circus pigeon, you know. I'm here on a very serious mission and I represent the highest authority in the park.' He landed on the man's hand and stood on one leg then the other.

'But the speech is coming from your beak, it's you speaking, you're speaking to me, you're a pigeon and you can talk.'

'Yes and it's a pity you can't. This is going to be hard work unless you snap out of it and accept that I can talk.' He was about to add that he could sing, too, but decided against that. 'Poison ... squirrels ... come on, talk to me.'

'You're the pigeon on my car, outside the taxidermist shop in Deptford.'

'That's me.'

'And now you want to talk about the poisoning of the squirrels.'

'Quite right ... but when you're ready of course, don't rush.'

'Yes, OK, and it'll probably be the most sensible discussion on the matter ever. Let me explain, there are too many grey squirrels in Greenwich Park. There's no disputing that point, everyone agrees.' He leaned back and Mr Tolly jumped from his hand onto the desk. 'The poisoning option wasn't mine; nobody in the park likes the idea. It's the council, they want results and they want them quick.'

'Tell me, how you'd prefer to overcome the problem of too many squirrels.'

'Natural predators, there aren't enough natural predators, you see. We need more hawks and owls.'

'... or the same number of hawks and owls eating more squirrels,' *'and less pigeons'* he thought.

'That would have the same net result, I suppose, although I don't see how birds of prey can be influenced in their diet.' He drummed his fingers on the desk and looked to the ceiling for inspiration. While he wasn't looking, Mr Tolly tried drumming with his toes.

'Unless,' he pushed himself out of the chair and paced around the office. 'Maybe if squirrels tasted better, they would have more appeal.' He paused at a stuffed grey squirrel and stared at it.

'How do you get them to stand still like that?' asked Mr Tolly.

'What do you mean?'

'All these animals and birds, look ... I can't do it, I keep falling over.'

'Oh, I see,' laughed the man, 'they're stuffed, they're dead. Beautiful aren't they?' He went on to explain that all of his collection died natural deaths and this was a way of preserving them for ever.

'Mm, I notice you don't have any pigeons ... don't get any ideas or I'll be off out of that window in a flash.'

'You needn't worry, I prefer living creatures' then pointing to the grey squirrel. 'How can I make grey squirrels tastier? That's the question.' He sat at the desk again and he seemed to ignore Mr Tolly. 'Sugar? No, too messy. Ketchup? Brown sauce? No, now I'm being silly. How on earth does one enhance the flavour of squirrels ... flavour enhancer of course, that's it! Instead of feeding the squirrels warfarin – feed them monosodium glutamate. It works on crisps ... why shouldn't it work on squirrels? Tell me that, Mr Tolly.'

But Mr Tolly had heard enough and flew to join his friends high in the tree.

He delivered a summary of his meeting with the foreman, he told of the over-population of squirrels and that poisoning would not be necessary if more of them were eaten by owls and other hunting birds.

The brave little troop of Ed the rat, the brothers Crispin and Alf, Elvis and headed up by Mr Tolly HO made their way to the ancient oak that housed the owl headquarters.

Emigration

Mr Tolly introduced Ed the rat and reminded Merlin of the promise of freedom of passage for him. Only then began the presentation of the case for *'squirrel slaughter by flavour enhancer'*.

Ed stood close to the exit in case he had to do a runner, which would not help a great deal as the only escape was straight along the broad beam towards a long fall and certain death. With the light behind him, his anxious glances went unnoticed.

The surprise came as Mr Tolly rounded off his presentation with the solution which involved owls and hawks changing their diets to squirrel meat. That instead of poison the park authorities would feed the squirrels with a substance that would enhance their flavour.

'I understand baby squirrels are particularly delicious, tender and nourishing, I've heard,' he concluded.

Ed spotted saliva glistening at the corners of the owls' beaks and was convinced that Mr Tolly had persuaded them ... until he saw Judy's dark glowering expression. The light from outside cast deep shadows, her eye sockets appearing hollow and empty.

'What you are suggesting is completely unacceptable. Eat baby squirrels? We're not animals, you know.'

The disappointment on the faces of Merlin and Bouncer was clear as they turned towards the crow.

'But,' began Bouncer, 'it's only natural, squirrels, mice, voles, rats, they're all part out natural diet, and we eat them already.'

'Yes, but what the pigeon is suggesting is focussing on squirrels, what then will happen to the mice, voles and rats? Do you want the park teeming with rats?'

'I'm sure that's not what Mr Tolly had in mind,' said Merlin, 'don't you mean, eat more squirrels? Especially those delicious baby ones, and you're right, they are very tender.'

Mr Tolly hadn't reckoned on opposition to his proposal nor was he very good at arguing his case quickly under pressure. So he suggested something that he regretted as soon as the words left his beak.

'Why don't we ask Edwina?'

'Yes,' agreed Judy, her hollow eyes turning towards Ed again, 'what a good idea, eh, Ed the rat?'

So, she asked the plastic doll, but the plastic did not respond.

'P ... per perhaps she's out,' said Ed, 'or laryngitis, there's a lot of laryngitis about, don't you know ... sore throats and that sort of thing.'

'Rubbish, enough of this, send for King Silver ... you two,' she pointed to Alf and Crispin, 'fetch King Silver, and be quick about it.'

'I'll help find him,' said Ed.

'No you won't, you stay exactly where you are.'

The uncomfortable silence was short-lived and the King of the squirrels arrived with three attendants.

Merlin, stepped in front of Judy obscuring her from view. He addressed King Silver, explaining the reason behind the poisoning proposition.

'... and so you see, there are too many grey squirrels.'

'Too many squirrels? Too many squirrels? How absurd, what do you mean? On whose authority? Where shall we go? What shall we do? We'll have to leave. We leave or die a death by poison.'

'Calm down Silver ... there is an alternative solution,' said Judy stepping out from Merlin's shadow.

'Who would like to explain it? Mr Tolly? Merlin? Bouncer? Or how about you, Ed the rat? You've a reputation for telling a good tale.'

But there were no volunteers, none of them were able to formulate an argument persuasive enough to convince Silver and his squirrels to stay ... to be eaten alive.

*

So, that very night the squirrels left. All of the grey squirrels of Greenwich Park made their way to the River Thames at Greenwich and took the first ship to America.

*

Mr Tolly could not wait to tell his friend the foreman the good news and, early the next morning he peered through the closed window of the office. The foreman was busy, there were large packing cases stacked in one corner and Mr Tolly watched as he carefully lowered the stuffed jay into a cardboard box.

He tapped at the glass with his beak and watched the man's face turn towards him. He marvelled at the change in the face as it focused through the window, the change from dark to light, as if, on seeing Mr Tolly, the sun shone, opening the mouth and wrinkling the soft skin around the eyes. The pigeon tried to imitate the movements as the window opened.

'Good morning, Mr Tolly. How are you?'

'How am I? I'm fine and I have some very good news.' He had prepared his speech on the wing and it would be dramatic with plenty of body movement.

'Good news, eh? That's just what I need because I'm afraid I've got some bad news, I've been sacked. They call it 'Early Retirement on Medical Grounds' but I've been booted out, fired. That's why I'm packing all my things, thirty years of looking after Greenwich Park and that's how the Council treats me.'

'But the squirrels have gone ... all of them. By the light of the moon, they left for America, by boat. They were seen by the night birds leaving through the bottom gate, heading for the River Thames. Won't the Council let you stay when they learn that?'

The foreman taped the flaps on the box carefully and then sat at his desk. Mr Tolly landed on the telephone and watched his face for movement. The darkness had returned.

'I don't think so, they've lost faith in me. First, my idea to feed flavour enhancer to the squirrels, I can see how stupid that was now, and I've been seen talking to my stuffed animals and birds. It must have been us talking together and, of course my explanation that I wasn't talking to stuffed animals but to a live pigeon just made matters worse. That's what comes from being honest.'

The foreman didn't really believe Mr Tolly's story about the squirrels leaving, he knew there were no boats to America from Greenwich Pier, but he didn't want to hurt his feelings, so said nothing to contradict him.

'I'm getting used to the idea of retirement and I'll still visit the park,' Mr Tolly watched the smile return to the man's face and he felt his own smile inside, 'and we can still meet and talk.'

'Where do you go when you aren't at the park? Do you have a nest beyond the walls? Perhaps I could visit you at your nest.'

Mr Tolly was at first alarmed by the laughter, he had seen and heard it before, but never this close. He jumped and landed again on the desk, embarrassed by his overreaction.

'Of course, you can visit me,' he stood up and walked to the window, 'follow that van this evening.' A white van waited outside the office.

*

So that mild May evening he followed the van through the streets to where the foreman lived. He watched from the roof of the van as his wife came to help with the boxes. Oddly, as they began speaking, Mr Tolly realised that he couldn't understand the conversation. The words meant nothing to him.

'I don't suppose you've heard the news about the Cutty Sark, have you?' she asked.

'What? Don't tell me it's burnt down again.'

'No, not quite that bad, it's been occupied by thousands of squirrels.'

The foreman's head turned in search of his pigeon friend, their eyes met and Mr Tolly saw the sun in his smile.

Judy

And so the grey squirrels of Greenwich Park eventually returned to their American roots.

King Silver's heart swelled with pride at having led the evacuation of his trusty troop of squirrels to Manhattan Island, in record time, too. His tail twitched as he focused on the nearing shoreline and his lungs filled with salty sea air, which induced a fit of coughing 'well, perhaps not so salty' he had to admit.

'This is North Woolwich – North Woolwich. Thank you for using the Woolwich Ferry. All vehicles must leave the ferry. Foot passengers, mind the step. This is North Woolwich.'

*

At owl HQ, Edwina sat in her usual spot and although she had nothing to say, her ears, ears of the rodent kind, monitored certain changes.

Merlin and Bouncer blinked towards the light, neither yet settled in their new role as leaders of the animals and birds. They had the power and the authority, but with the squirrel problem over, they lacked direction of any sort. The squirrel saga had all too easily fallen into place with hardly any intervention from the owl brothers, indeed, at times they struggled to be heard. Judy seemed to have guided the situation to a satisfactory solution with the help of Mr Tolly and now, with nothing to react to, they felt redundant.

They had been dozing all day. Now evening approached, they woke, blinked a little and gazed drowsily across the park.

'Has the park employed a new foreman yet?' asked Merlin for the sake of saying something.

'Nobody knows, but Mr Tolly and his crew are keeping an eye on things,' replied Bouncer, adding, 'I don't understand how those pigeons can befriend a rat and a sparrow hawk. The world has gone mad. There used to be a time when "birds of a feather flocked together".'

'You could apply the same argument to us owls and Judy the crow. Sometimes cooperation is complementary to all parties. One often sees it in human behaviour.'

'Yes, you could be right Merlin. You could be right.'

'All this talk of *'birds of a feather'* is making me hungry. It has been a long day and evening is nigh. Food time!' The owl brothers waddled out onto the broad branch and flew their different ways into the evening air.

*

Ed had made some improvements to his spy den. Alf and Crispin had collected twigs which he wove into a platform, creating a floor by pushing some of the longer twigs into the soft lining of the walls. He then carpeted it with dried moss and leaves from the park. Cosy, and no more sitting on that sharp saddle. He had noticed that, since Old Owl's demise, the nest remained mostly unoccupied. Bouncer and Merlin had their own nests, with young owlets that required their attention and the HQ was just that – a place for meetings and court sessions. He had to be careful not to be caught sleeping on the job.

There was a young rat named Ed
Who was thinking of going to bed
'This rat's not for dinner
So, sleep tight, Edwina
And don't snore or I'll end up dead'.

Ed dreamed sweet dreams of flying like a bird with Alf and Crispin, of his old life in the house with Mr Noon and Russell. And of rat poison.

He awoke with a start. He could hear voices, not owl voices either. It was crows – Judy and some of her crow friends – he could not discern exactly how many, but he recognised Judy's *"caw caw"*.

'This is the place, and the first thing to go is that doll. Owls have a stupid sentimentality about such things and an unrealistic notion that they are wiser than humans. Wisdom is one thing, cunning is another. Time and events will judge which of the two is superior. And then there will be change. Oh yes, there are going to be some changes around Greenwich Park. And it will start and finish with a war.'

The crows walked out of earshot onto the beam and Ed could hear no more of the conversation.

'I had better warn Merlin and Bouncer. But that can wait.' Food was on his mind, his empty stomach rumbled. He didn't have to wait long before Alf and Crispin came and flew him to the troughs in the deer enclosure.

'Lads, there is something Merlin and Bouncer must be made aware of, something very serious, too, and I think Edwina's going to tell them. Fly me to my secret den, lads – Edwina is going to be busy.'

But HQ was deserted. Ed had a snooze in his den while Alf and Crispin flew to fetch the owl brothers.

He was awoken by the voices of Judy and Bouncer.

'So you don't know what triggered all the chanting?' said Judy.

'I hadn't really thought about it. I imagined it came from a general assumption that Merlin should be the new 'Old Owl'.

'And it didn't concern you that there was no vote, no debate, no chance for any other owl – or any other bird for that matter to put themselves forward for the leadership?'

'No.'

'And it doesn't concern you that Merlin may have started the chanting? That the groundswell of support – the whole shift of power was rigged?'

'Don't talk like that. Why are you asking me all these questions? What are you suggesting?'

'I'm suggesting that you had an equal right to be considered for the role. Who is it that provides the muscle when it is needed? Who took charge when the Royal Egg had to be transported? Who physically bore the weight and accepted the grave responsibility for the task? Bouncer – that's who. Bouncer – Bouncer – Bouncer. So why was the chant "Merlin"? Did you never ponder that conundrum?'

'Get out. It is as it is. Now shoo.' He chased her out of the nest and along the beam catching her tail feathers in his beak.

She took to the air. Had her bone-hard beak been able to smirk – it would have smirked.

*

The next morning Merlin arrived at HQ determined to be more proactive. 'Mm no Ed the rat and no Judy. Good morning Bouncer, Mr Tolly, Crispin, Alf, Elvis and Mercedes.' He nodded to each of them.

'We can't wait for the others. So, Mr Tolly, do we know who the new foreman is going to be?'

Compared to the historic event of the Royal Egg and the drama of the squirrel crisis, the 'new foreman situation' paled into insignificance. Merlin was not really interested, he doubted that it would impact on the park's wildlife, but perhaps statesmanship had its tedium as well as its excitement.

'There isn't going to be one. I hear that a committee from the council is to run the park. No foreman.'

'That's odd,' said Bouncer. 'As far as I can remember there has always been a foreman.'

'Keep an eye on developments, Mr Tolly,' said Merlin.

'I will, the old foreman and I meet periodically and he updates me.'

'Good. I wonder where Judy is, I haven't seen her for a while.'

'Judy seeks power. There will be calm – but it will be the calm before the storm.'

The heads turned to face Edwina. Even Mr Tolly had to remind himself that it was Ed speaking the words, and shocking words at that, he thought 'What does Ed know that we don't?' he thought.

'Beware of the dark. Beware of the dark.'

*

When Merlin returned to his nest both chicks were missing. He searched the floor at the base of the tree and found them dead. He flew to Bouncer's nest. Bouncer's mate had fought off an attack by crows.

'*Beware of the dark,*' said Bouncer.

'*The calm before the storm*' said Merlin.

Bouncer recounted his confrontation with Judy.

'She tried to drive a wedge between us, she suggested that I should have been the new Old Owl. And I have to confess that for one very brief moment, I felt a strange ... it was as if I wanted to be leader ... which I've never wanted ... I experience hate towards my brother ... there must a word for it ... it was a feeling that perhaps only humans can properly describe ... perhaps they have a word for it.'

'Humans have words for most things. But your earlier comments – about "birds of a feather" may have come home to roost. Perhaps Old Owl's idea of bringing Judy into our confidence has turned sour. I see it more clearly now. Old Owl's obsessional focus on the safe transition of the Royal Egg and her desire to boost our team with Judy's brain power has exposed us and left us vulnerable.'

He looked at the moon as it broke the cloud cover.

'Kill the messenger,' said Merlin.

'The messenger was clearly Mr Tolly,' said Bouncer.

'But perhaps the words themselves became twisted over those hundred years – thousand years. Perhaps Judy should have been the one killed. It was wise of Old Owl to spare Mr Tolly.'

'Merlin, you must call a council of war. When the dawn chorus announces the new day we must meet. All of us – pigeons, rat and sparrow hawk. Judy must be destroyed,' said Bouncer.

'Spoken like a true leader. We meet at dawn.'

*

They gathered as the sun pushed the moon to where it hides during the day. They waited on the beam for the late-comers before entering the nest.

'We can't find Ed. He must be asleep somewhere,' said Crispin.

Merlin and Bouncer entered the nest first. Where the doll normally sat was a vacant space. Edwina had gone. In the wall behind – a large hole.

They stood in silence. Pigeon eyes adjusted to the dark, Elvis and Mr Tolly walked to the hole and saw Ed's conker dangling on its string. Alf and Crispin flew to the base of the tree and, sure enough, Edwina lay face down in the undergrowth.

'Do you think the crows have killed Ed the rat?' said Alf.

'Probably. I think Judy knew all along that it wasn't the doll that did the speaking,' said Crispin.

'Poor Ed, I will miss him.'

'Psst.'

'What was that?'

'It must have been the wind.'

'Pssssst.'

'No, listen, it's coming from the other side of the tree.' They skirted the tree trunk.

'Psst. It's me, Ed. Get me out of here.'

Alf and Crispin giggled when they saw the familiar snout protruding from a gap between the massive roots.

'What about those rat teeth you were telling us about the other day "chew through anything these rat teeth", you said.'

'I'm sure if we placed a little rat poison on the grass here you would be out of there like lightning,' said Crispin. The pigeon brothers returned to the nest.

'Edwina has been dropped into the undergrowth below,' said Crispin.

'We guessed as much.' Said Merlin. 'Bouncer can you retrieve her? Then we have to plan a strategy.'

'I'll fetch her now, I can't bear to think of Edwina treated in that disrespectful manner.'

Elvis and Mr Tolly glanced at each other but decided not to draw attention to the hole in the wall, or the conker on the string, or the suspended floor, or the rat droppings.

In a short while, Edwina sat in her usual place – her two eyes open.

'Here's a summary of the situation,' began Merlin. 'It seems Judy is leading the crows in an all-out offensive against an owl regime, which has held power since the beginning of time. Judy has been among us, and became a useful ally during the period of the recovery of the Royal Egg. But she has betrayed our trust and must die. Kill Judy and the uprising will be quelled. Does any of you disagree?'

'What about the baby?' said Mr Tolly.

'What baby?' said Merlin.

'The human baby from the Royal Egg, Baby Blue. I remember Old Owl saying that although our duty of care is over, we would observe it from afar, or something like that I can't exactly …'

'You're right, Mr Tolly. I hadn't thought about the human baby. Do you think Judy would harm it?'

Elvis said. 'Judy has struck at the heart of owl culture by raiding its headquarters and disrespecting Edwina. She has killed your owlets, I think she's capable of anything.'

'But harm a human baby?' said Bouncer. 'It's us she wants to damage.'

'Us and our power source. She knows the secret of the Royal Egg. Kill the baby, outwit us owls and her species has a clear hundred year run. We need to guard the baby. Where is it? Does anyone know where its nest is?'

No one did.

'I have spoken with the human baby, in the park, but I don't know where it nests.' said Mr Tolly.

Mr Tolly recounted the episode when the baby sent him to speak with the foreman about the squirrel problem.

'Why don't we ask Edwina?' said Bouncer.

'Or even better, the Chosen One – Helen,' said Crispin glancing at the gaping hole behind the doll, 'she's bound to know.'

'Fly, Mr Tolly, fly. Mercedes, please accompany him for protection.'

'Protection? A sparrow hawk? Come on then Mercedes, but don't get any culinary ideas on the way.'

'Don't flatter yourself Mr Tolly.'

'We're outnumbered that is our biggest drawback,' continued Merlin. 'We have no way of knowing how many troops Judy has at her disposal. It may be only a dozen or so close followers, but if it's the whole of the crow population of Greenwich Park ...'

'Plus the rooks and magpies ...'

'And the jays ...'

'We need to know,' concluded Merlin.

'Know what? What do you need to know?' It was Ed the rat. He had rose to the challenge and gnawed a gap just big enough for him to escape. Alf and Crispin flew him to the nest and he stood at the opening, blinking into the dark.

Merlin updated him on the news. If anyone could advise on espionage it was Ed the rat.

'That's easy. If these crows are so keen to take over this place, then let 'em. I've discovered a network of tunnels behind all that solid looking woodwork there. Vacate the place, move Edwina to a new nest, you must be able to find a suitable residence nearby. Then conceal a spy somewhere in this labyrinth of tunnels. Easy.'

'How do you know all that?' asked Bouncer.

'I'm a rat. One of the most successful species ever. It's my destiny to know these things. Another point – I wouldn't like to call this place home if we had one of those terrible storms. Now is a good time to move if you don't mind me saying.'

'Sound advice wouldn't you say, Bouncer?'

'Mm, it's a good idea, but where do we find a spy we can trust?'

*

Mr Tolly and Mercedes alighted in the tree overlooking Helen's garden. A family party was in progress to celebrate the twins' fifth birthday. They were all there, including Mark and Lucy and the baby twins.

Mr Tolly experienced the now familiar vibrating and received a message from Blue.

'Listen to the humans, you'll be able to understand them.'

Lucy spoke. 'First it was just a couple of crows in the trees, but then I found a magpie actually in the pram. I chased it off before it could do any harm, but it worried me. They carry diseases.'

'Magpies are attracted to shiny items, perhaps it had seen one of the chrome buttons on the pram cover,' said Andy.

'You can buy cat nets to keep cats away,' said Helen's mum.

'Or buy a cat to keep the birds away,' said Helen.

'We have one, a cat net that is,' she said 'and I've started to use it, but it doesn't keep germs out. I've stopped leaving the twins alone in the garden until they're a little older.'

Mr Tolly beckoned Mercedes to follow him to the far side of the tree. He translated the eavesdropped conversation.

'We shall wait and follow them to where they nest, from there we can watch over the twins.'

*

Merlin, Bouncer, Alf and Crispin volunteered Ed the rat as 'spy-in-chief'. New headquarters were found in the dense ivy which clad the Greenwich Observatory and Edwina had views across London.

*

It wasn't too long before Ed had traced his original journey from the top to the bottom of the oak tree. At those places where the tunnel ran close to the bark – and he gleaned this by tapping and listening – he gnawed a tiny window for the light to shine through.

Around the nest proper he worked listening cells big enough for him to rest comfortably and without it being too claustrophobic.

'It's a great pity I can't show off my masterpiece labyrinth to anyone. But that's the irony of espionage, I suppose.'

A famous young rat 'spy-in-chief'
Was notorious from park to heath
The maize that he chewed
Powered the maze which he hewed
But he hoped his employment was brief.

*

First one, then rapidly four more, crows crashed into the windscreen of Marks car as he drove his family home. The toughened glass withstood the impact and Mark pulled up onto the pavement.

*

The family car, cleared of dead crows, made it home and Mr Tolly and Mercedes flew to HQ to report the incident.

'Where is everyone? Where's Edwina? The place is deserted.'

'Oh no it isn't. The spy-in-chief is at home.'

'Ed, where are Merlin and Bouncer? We have news.'

'They've moved to a new nest and taken Edwina with them. And no, I don't know where it is, but you had better hop it. I'm expecting the new residents soon.'

Mercedes watched over Baby Blue's house and Mr Tolly sought out Crispin and Alf who led him to the new headquarters.

*

At the new nest, Mr Tolly awaited Merlin's reaction to the news of the kamikaze crows.

'Good work, Mr Tolly. Good work. The war has begun. The enemy has made all the moves, so far. The raiding of Old Owl's nest – the murder of my owlets – the attack on Baby Blue in his pram and now the kamikaze attack on the car.

We have Judy precisely where we want her. She thinks she has an advantage, she will have interpreted our retreat from the old nest as a victory. Occupying Old Owls inner sanctum will appeal to her vanity, her intellectual pride will be in overload – but her death approaches – and approaches fast.

At midnight, Bouncer and I will visit our cousins at the cemetery. We require the bag, the bag which bore the Royal Egg. We need it to carry some weaponry. And one more thing, Mr Tolly, you shall ask a favour of your good friend the foreman.'

'I can try. What sort of favour?'

'Come close. No other creature must hear this ...'

In whispers Merlin outlined his devious plan for the downfall of Judy.

*

The guard on Baby Blue was quadrupled – another sparrow hawk and two kestrels.

The canvas bag was retrieved from the base of the old oak tree. A net large enough to cover the entrance to the old nest was scavenged from the workshop and pigeon power could be left to Elvis to arrange. There were plenty of pigeons willing to thank him for their freedom.

*

At midnight, Merlin and Bouncer, in the tranquillity of the cemetery, balanced on headstones and spoke with their cousins.

'Five or six should be sufficient, and make it clear that there's some risk but the reward will be great.'

'And you want them in this bag? And all being well, they'll be returned in the bag?'

'That's the intention. Oh, and, if possible, make it a selection of your most highly toxic. It's all for a good cause.'

'It sounds like it. I'll see what I can do. Wait here.'

'It's quite interesting that humans put there dead ones into the ground, don't you think?' said Bouncer.

'Interesting yes, and appropriate that those at the top of the food chain should return to nourish those at the bottom. Don't you think?'

'Yes. An amusing hypothesis. And had owls been blessed with a sense of humour, we would most likely be laughing now.'

*

The setting of the trap had to be swift and secretive. Merlin and Bouncer directed operations from the new nest in the silent company of Edwina.

From his escape hole at the base of the oak, Ed confirmed that Judy had not yet made her approach and that the old nest remained vacant.

Three sparrow hawks and two buzzards cleared the area of crows and then stood guard.

It took less than a few minutes to set the trap. With great reverence, the stuffed effigy of Old Owl was placed at the exact spot which Edwina used to occupy.

The contents of the bag – six vipers, were concealed in Ed's former hiding place behind Old Owl.

Petroc and seven racing pigeons waited with the net. Mr Tolly signalled the buzzards and sparrow hawks to withdraw and he hid with Petroc and co.

It would be Mr Tolly's responsibility to confirm that it was definitely Judy who had entered the trap. Crows are similar in appearance and Merlin had reckoned that she might send in some foot soldiers to spring any possible trap.

Ed would signal to the vipers when to strike. He peeped through a little hole and the mid-morning sun shone in on the empty nest.

The sun rose in the sky and the shadows shifted. Ed yawned and he lay down.

His body stiffened at the sound of activity on the beam outside. At his spy hole again he saw a lone black head waddle towards the opening. The bird stopped and leaned forward. Ed could see that it wasn't Judy. The crow screamed in alarm at the sight of Old Owl and retreated in great haste.

The church bell from across the heath struck one. Petroc and his team waited restlessly with the net.

Three crows approached in formation through the air.

'That's Judy. The one at the front,' whispered Mr Tolly.

Ed's beady eye registered them as they landed and he recognised the target.

Judy strutted arrogantly into the late Old Owl's domain.

'What on earth are you talking about? Old Owl is dead. I'm surrounded by imbeciles, out of the way, let me see. Old Owl is dead, I assure you, I witnessed her death – she can't possibly ...'

She stopped.

She stood motionless.

She stared across the nest waiting for Old Owl to blink or utter a sound, but Old Owl's glass eyes stared blindly ahead, and, as if her wisdom had survived her death, her beak remained tightly closed.

Judy heard the sound of the approaching racing pigeons.

She heard Ed's whistle screeching through his teeth.

She heard the hissing from the back of the viper's throats, she saw the pink mouths gaping wide and the strands of lethal saliva.

Petroc's team held the net in place – there was no escape. Fangs penetrated first feathers then flesh. Toxin pumped from glands. Wings beat. Legs jumped. Poison paralysed muscles, wing muscles, leg muscles – and hearts.

***

'You see, it pays to be quick.' Dappled sun beams warmed Ed as he lay on the roof of his nest box just as he used to. Alf and Crispin listened attentively – Ed's tales were always worth listening to.

'I didn't know that Judy and her mob had slung Edwina out of the nest. How was I to know? I was prattling on, *"Beware of the dark, beware of the dark. Trouble is a-brewing ..."* when suddenly the wall caved in. I looked up and there was her beak coming at me like a black spear.'

A rat to survive must be speedy
Strong and virile not weedy
So resist food that's poisonous
Even when you're ravenous
And you'll never find yourself needy.

10579843R00065

Printed in Great Britain
by Amazon